THE
MAIDEN VOYAGE
OF THE
FALCON

**Written and illustrated
by
G. E. Stevens.**

Mathetes Publishing,
34, North Hill Rd., Ipswich, Suffolk, England, IP4 2PN.
Telephone: 01473 210765.
Email:george35stevens@btinternet.com

**THE
MAIDEN VOYAGE
OF THE
FALCON**

ISBN 978-0-9557881-1-6

First published in 2007.

To the children of Class 2,
Raby St. Primary School, 1981.

Contents.

Chapters and Titles.

1.   "Be not drunk with wine."
2.   "But he knoweth the way that I take."
3.   "Be strong and of good courage."
4.   "A wise man will hear and will increase learning."
5.   "Enter not into the path of the wicked."
6.   "Who so diggeth a pit shall fall therein."
7.   "Faithful are the wounds of a friend."
8.   "A merry heart doeth good like a medicine, but..."
9.   "Perfect love casteth out fear..."
10.   "A good name is chosen rather than great riches."
11.   "All things work together for good to them that love God..."

CHAPTER 1
"Be not drunk with wine" Ephesians 5:18.

The evening shadows lengthened in the doorways of New York. Creaking planks signalled a cooling breeze and the light from flickering oil lamps danced in the alleyways. A lithe form, black as raven, swept into one such passage. It paused beneath an oil lamp and turned its head to look behind. Its eyes twinkled. Quickly and silently, it skipped and faded into the shadow of a doorway. Following the creature was a faint song that crescendoed as its maker turned into the alley.

"Whisky is the life of man,
Whisky Johnny.
Oh, whisky is the life of man,
Whisky for my Johnny."
The strains ceased as the drunkard staggered into the lamplight revealing an oval, red face that was carelessly crowned with a dinted bowler. Gently, he swayed backwards and forwards.

"Them's were the days," spat from his threadlike lips, "rockin' 'n' rollin' 'n' racin' 'board a fine clipper ship. Ah, them's were the days."

He bent towards the light. His eyes were peering, narrow slits. The flask in his right hand glinted as he bent backward to present it to the flame. "Cheers to 'e," he toasted. Immediately, he placed it to his lips and gulped several mouthfuls of its contents.

"Aah," he approved. With a hic of contentment, the drunkard leaned back onto rough timbers. Broken strains of "Blow the Man Down" saw him slip slowly down the wall to sit like a rag doll on the dry earth. Bloodshot eyes closed. Whisky gurgled from the tilted flask. Soon silence emphasised only the loud snores that shook the head of his limp body.

Suddenly, "Jaaacko," hauntingly poked the peace. "Jaacko Crocker." The inebriated man opened his eyes widely, lifted his head, leaned forward, looked right, looked left, looked up, looked down, deliberately scratched his head under his bowler, grunted, and then resumed his snoozing position.

Several snores passed before the same voice again spooked the silence… "I've 'ad me eye on ye for a long time now, Jacko Crocker."

Jack Crocker awoke with a start. Clumsily, he dropped onto all fours. Then he rose to his knees. The effects of liquor swaying his shoulders, he clutched his hat to his chest and lifted his eyes skywards.

"Are 'e the devil or the Lord?" he cried. He listened. Then he mumbled, "Makes no diff'rence. Either way, I've 'ad it."

The dark shape lunged forward hissing its reply. "It be the devil, Jacko. Come to get what ye owes 'im."

Cold steel thudded into the neck of Crocker, whose cry of pain was cut short as a tough hand was clamped across his mouth. Jack Crocker grew dizzier as he fought for breath. The bowler hat fell from his grasp and rolled away. Suddenly, the hand moved from his face to his hair and pulled. Swooning, the drunkard gasped, "Devil ye are not! Beast ye are! Human…"

"Cut yer cackle!" peppered the air. "Now hand over that there paper 'bout yer neck!"

Crocker started. His face paled to marble. Even in his drunken state, he knew that this was no ordinary thief. He wondered who could know about that paper. Playing for time, he bluffed, "Paper! What paper?"

The pistol barrel bolted into his neck. The twist on his hair sharply tightened until his head was exploding with the pain. Clearly, the beast was angry, "Don't play games with me, Jingler. Hand it over."
Through his stupor and pain the whisky lover knew that there was something unusual about that order. It struck him in a flash that lit up the name "Jingler".

"Jingler! Only one man ever called I that. Ye're -" Crocker's revelation was interrupted by starry pain as his head was struck. The dust choked him as his face dug into the ground. His head swam in a sea of darkness and light. Rough fingers clawed at his collar. He was helpless. Thin leather bit into his throat as the pouch was ripped from about his neck. Pain tore into his back as a heavy boot stamped and pressed upon it. The thief deftly opened the leather bag and removed a paper. It crackled open as he lifted it

high into the lamplight. While he did so, the victim's senses began to return more soberly. His mind planned escape. He listened.

"A fine title to a bit o' property, this be," purred the robber.

"Ye 'ave what ye came for," declared the choking man. "Now, what d'ye intend doin' with I?"

Immediately, he wished he had never spoken for the load lifted from his back and a boot sliced into his side.

"Now, there be a problem, m'hearty," replied the plunderer, "but seein' yer down there lookin' for the devil, I might as well send ye to 'im."

The sobered drunk winced as he heard a spine-chilling laugh and the gun's hammer cock. He waited for a shot.

Unexpectedly, a cry smothered the crack of the revolver, "HELP! MURDER!" The bullet splattered the dirt in front of the victim's face. The robber thudded to earth with a young lad wrestling him. Crocker looked round. Again the shout erupted, "MURDER! HE -." It was cut short as the gun's barrel whipped the boy's skull.

Jackson Crocker took his chance. He struggled up to face his enemy. With a yelp, he attacked. His arms were high and his fingers were talons.

"Oh, no yer don't, Jingler!" ripped out the thief. Another shot exploded. One man fell. Jackson Crocker was dead. The plunderer moved quickly. He examined his prey just to be sure. "Dead." His mind raced on, "Crocker's dead - good. The boy - out cold. The paper - gone. Where's that paper?" he hissed, scanning the area. A distant shout pushed his haste. Someone was coming. He must find the document.

The voices were coming closer. "This way lads. The shots came from over here."

The boy stirred. The eyes of the murderer spotted the paper in the boy's hand. He leaped across, snatched at it, and hearing, "There he is, lads. Down the alley!" he fled into the night.

Three men thumped past as the boy slowly regained his senses and balance. Lifting his hand to his aching head, he noticed some paper clinging to it. Drowsily, he slipped it into his pocket and leaned on the wall. His legs felt like thin sticks arched to breaking point. Hearing boots striding, he looked up. Entering the light and his hazy vision was a man. The lad noted his average height, grey shirt, dark trousers and leather waistcoat. A twinkle glanced from his chest.

"Must be the law," thought the lad. He was right. The lawman knelt beside the body of Jack Crocker levelling the rifle at his head - just in case.

"Dead. Dead as a Christmas turkey," he declared. The officer let the dead arm drop. He turned his pale eyes to the boy, rose up and putting his hands on his shoulder, asked, "You all right, son?"

"I - I reckon. Just a bit dazed," replied the youth, simultaneously taking stock of the deputy's gaunt features and bristly chin.

"D'you think you could tell me what happened?"

Sandy Scott's memory rehearsed the events quickly. "I think so," he began, "but I didn't see much."

"Now just take your time, lad. Think hard."

"Well, I was passing the end of the alley there," he related, thumbing in its direction, "when I heard voices. I looked down the alley and spotted that fellow there, lying on the ground. Another man was standing over him and pointing a pistol at him."

"What did the other chap look like?" interrupted the deputy.

"Let's see. He wore a black, wide-brimmed hat and a dark cape. His face was masked with a chequered neckerchief." Sandy paused. He could think of nothing else.

"What about his voice, lad?"

"I didn't really hear his voice, but he did laugh just before I tackled him. A chilling kind of laugh it was. Not the kind you'd forget in a hurry."

At that moment, two men stepped out from the darkness. The deputy swivelled and pointed his rifle toward them. The taller one raised his right hand. The lawman, recognising them, lowered his weapon.

"Any luck, Bob?" he asked.

"No, Jim. He showed us a clean pair of heels."

The officer sighed. Bob nodded towards the body.

"Dead," said Jim. "I haven't searched him yet though."

The comrades squatted over the still man and rummaged through his pockets. They discovered a key, a large handkerchief embroidered with the initials "J.C.," a small box of cigars and a leather wallet full of dollars. Jim wrapped these into his bandanna and added the empty pouch that he had found close to the corpse.

"Well, it don't seem that robbery were his motive, Jim," stated Bob.

"I'm not so sure," came the reply. "The pouch might've had something valuable in it."

The two men nodded at the possibility. "Better take the meat to the Black Hat, lads," suggested Jim. His companions reached under the dead arms and lifted the body. Then, pulling the arms over their shoulders, they started off in the direction of the mortuary. The boots of the corpse engraved two lines in the dust.

The deputy addressed Sandy, "You'd better come along with me, lad."

The boy visibly winced. "Where to?" he asked.

"Marshal's off -" began the deputy.

Sandy shot away like a bullet.

"Oi, lad! Come back here," called Jim, starting after him.   The others turned clumsily.

"You'll not catch him, Jim. He's like a hare," laughed Bob.

The lawman turned and headed towards them. Then his eyes widened. "Of course!" he blurted. "Fair hair, blue eyes, sprightly, wearing dark cords, white-sleeved shirt and beige waistcoat. That lad is the runaway from the orphanage."

"Reckon you're right there," agreed Bob.

"Yep," smiled Slim. "Let's get to the Marshal and tell him the tale of the two that got away."

The officer lifted dead legs and led the four into the darkness.

Chapter 2
"But He knoweth the way that I take" Job 23:10.

Meanwhile, in Main Street a signboard creaked as it swung in the breeze. A dull, orange glow widened from a nearby window to highlight its golden lettering. Inside the office below it sat a middle-aged, bespectacled gentleman. His hair was dark and wavy, but greyed where it bordered his square face. His sideburns reached down to link with his well-combed moustache and form a shallow "w" under his pitted nose. With a pen he scratched his signature on the bottom of a contract.

"Well, that's that," he uttered. "One contract requiring but one signature."

Sweeping the paper to one side, he stood and simultaneously smacked the polished wood with his left hand. Henry Daniels then reached for the folded newspaper that lay on the corner of his desk. He read it aloud as he paced the floor. His voice was touched with glee.

"Palmer was ever a captain to drive his ship and crew, yet safely. His last record run from New York to Valparaiso in sixty-nine days pushed the ship Sea Hawk to an average speed of seven knots. He had already achieved fifty days from Callao to Canton, averaging nine knots. Captain Palmer certainly deserves the praise of New York City for such a magnificent achievement. However, it is rumoured that Palmer wishes to swallow the anchor. What a tragedy this would be."

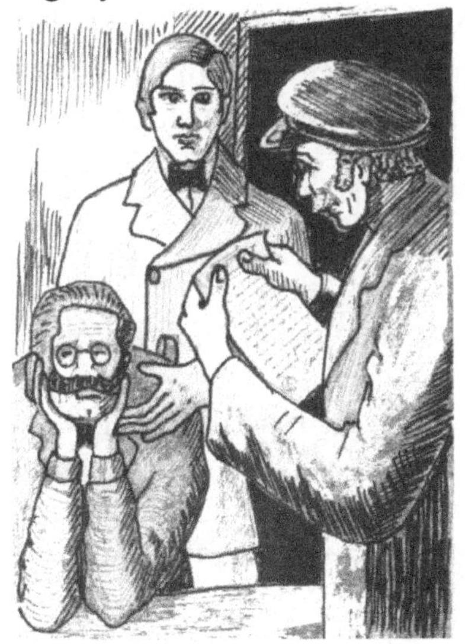

Daniels slapped the journal onto the desktop. "Swallow the anchor indeed," he grunted. "I'm sure the Falcon will change his mind for him."

Footsteps clattered on the boards outside. The heads of two men appeared above the curtain line that stretched across the window.

"It's them!" exclaimed Daniels striding across to open the door. Young Chuck Daniels, a tall, well-dressed fellow, entered first. His brown eyes gleamed. The other man seemed to be a giant. A black cap perched upon his head and a heavy, black coat dropped to just below his knees.

"Well, Henry, he's looked her over," chimed Chuck.

Henry enthusiastically shook the rough hand of the stranger, asking, "And what did you think of her Captain Palmer?"

Palmer removed his pipe from between full lips, puffed out blue smoke and replied in deep tones, "As a ship, sir, she's one of the finest clippers as

I've set me eyes upon, but -"

"But what, Captain?" interjected the ship's owner.

"Well, sir, I had me heart set on leaving the sea and starting a farm somewhere."

"You mean to say that seeing the Falcon hasn't changed your mind. You won't make just one more voyage to San Francisco?"

The ageing man turned to sit at his desk. His elbows supported the hands that cradled his head. His features expressed his disappointment.

"Don't get me wrong, sir," answered Palmer. "It ain't only that. It's a couple o' things. For a start, I know the mate's having trouble rounding up the last of the crew, and I've a shivering in me spine that I don't like."

Henry Daniels turned to Chuck. "Why is the mate having trouble completing the crew, Chuck?" he queried.

The younger brother hesitated, glanced at Palmer, and then addressed his partner. "It's because of superstition."

"SUPERSTITION! What d'you mean?"

The youngster shifted uncomfortably. "There are rumours flying around saying that we launched the Falcon with a bottle of water instead of champagne."

"And what if we did?" said Daniels, raising his eyebrows.

"I'll answer that one, if you don't mind, young sir," interrupted the captain.

The youngster nodded. Palmer continued, "Most ships that I know of Mr. Daniels - that have been launched with water that is, have been jinxed… cursed! That's why sensible men are 'feared to sail in one. Such ships are doomed from the start."

"Are you afraid, Captain Palmer?" challenged old Daniels.

Matthew Palmer silently gazed at the seated man. He knew what he knew, and it couldn't be coincidence.

Chuck broke in, "Captain Palmer, before you make your final decision, will you examine the contract?"

Palmer nodded. The document was passed to him. He read it thought-fully. He then whistled, long and low.

"As you can see, Captain, we can certainly make it worth your while. Those must be the best wages ever offered to any clipper's captain," added Chuck.

"You're right enough there, young sir. It's three times my last wage."

Daniels, seeing his chance, stood abruptly, and throwing out appealing hands, said, 'Now wouldn't that tidy sum fulfil your dream of a farm, Captain? Only one more voyage."

"Why are you willing to pay me so much?" asked the colossus. "What's the catch?"

For the first time the ship owner was momentarily caught off guard. His eyes darkened before he replied.

"Catch? Why, Captain, there is no catch. All we ask is that you get to San Francisco as quickly as possible."

Matt Palmer put his pipe into his mouth. He puffed smoke towards the ceiling as he considered the proposition. He was certainly curious and wondered how these two men were going to use him. Removing the pipe, he submitted, "Mmm. It's against my better judgement, but if you'll guarantee me a crew of fifty able-bodied seamen besides ordinary seamen and boys, I'll take you up on it."

The eyes of the ship owner twinkled, and his lips twitched into a faint smile. "It's a deal!" he said.

"Where's the pen then?" asked Palmer.

Daniels inked the pen and offered it to him. "You'll not regret signing, Captain. The Falcon's a record-breaking ship."

The captain signed and returned the pen. His face was stern.

"Don't expect records, sir. Not without a good crew and a healthy blow from above." Admonished, the ship owner gave the Falcon's master the details relating to the voyage. He concluded by telling the captain that he should use his initiative concerning the return trip and its cargo. They shook hands and the seafarer left. Henry Daniels turned to his young brother.

"Well, Chuck, it looks as though we might win the wager with the O'Connors now… a hundred thousand dollars. Just think of it."

Chuck was saddened by his brother's greed. "And what if Palmer doesn't beat the record?" he asked. "We'll go bust, won't we?"

The ship owner waved the question to one side and turned to look out of the window. "No. If he gets there, we'll still be all right."

Captain Palmer, however, had halted at the end of an alleyway to rekindle his pipe. He reflected upon the evening's events as he sucked. Suddenly, Sandy darted out from the darkness, and ran straight into the seaman. As the boy rebounded, the hand of Palmer clamped across his arm. Sandy uttered his apologies and tried, in vain, to pull free. The Captain, thinking the lad was a pickpocket, ordered, "Be still now while I check me pockets." The boy realised that he was being taken for a pickpocket. Angered by the accusation, Sandy tugged harder.

"I'm not a thief!" he barked. "I don't pick pockets."

"Well, at least you seem to be telling the truth," admitted Palmer examining his last pocket. "Everything's here - so why are you running?"

Sandy remained silent. He wondered whether or not to bite the hand that held him.

"No answer, eh? So how about me taking you home to your mum?"

Sandy fumed, "You can't."

"And why not?"

"Cause she's dead. That's why! So's my dad."

Matt Palmer relaxed his grip. The boy was upset. His head throbbed as tears seeped into his eyes.

"Ease up lad. I'm sorry," said the Captain. "I wasn't to know, was I?"

The sailor offered the boy his handkerchief. Sandy took it and blew his nose.

"Where are you staying?"

Sandy paused. He considered the man in front of him. Then he replied, "Orphanage. But I ain't going back to that place."

"Why ever not, lad? Do they beat you there?"

"Only when we deserve it."

"Then why won't you go back?"

"'Cause I'm too old. The rest of the kids are just young uns. I want to get out working."

The Captain pulled at his pipe as he examined the boy. He was short, but strong. He had been well brought up and seemed healthy.

"How old are you, boy?"

"Fourteen."

"Mm," pondered Palmer again removing his pipe. "Of a good age, eh. Ever thought of going to sea?"

Sandy's eyes widened. "Have I!" he exclaimed. "It's been my greatest dream to sail on one of them tall ships which fly to China like birds. It'd be hard work, but worth it."

Noting his enthusiasm, Palmer made him a proposition. "Well, lad, I'm the captain of the new clipper ship, Falcon. She's down at the quay opposite Maiden Lane. If you want to work that badly, sign on early the day after tomorrow and climb aboard."

Sandy was amazed. "You're a real captain? And you'll take me on board?"

"I am, and will, boy – on one condition."

"What's that?"

The captain poked his pipe towards the boy. "You go back to the orphanage and tell them about your dream. Then settle any other business you have before you sail."

Sandy hardly hesitated. He grabbed the captain's hand and said, "It's a deal, Captain, and thank you." Immediately, he turned and leapt away, shouting, "YIPPEE! YIPPEE!"

Matthew Palmer smiled, thought for a moment, shook his head and grunted, "Aach, Palmer, you're a sentimental old fool." He ambled on his way.

The waters of the rising tide splashed against the stalwart timbers supporting the pebbled quayside. Long, blue shadows heralded the rising sun whose light rippled white upon the waves. Hulls, many and varied, bobbed in the harbour. Sails sniffed the slight wind and quickened. Pulleys pulsed. Gaffs gargled as they climbed the masts. Chains champed. Raucous orders accentuated the discord.

The quayside was as lively as a disturbed colony of ants. Sailors slunk under heavy cargoes. Businessmen jostled to obtain the best buys of fish, vegetables and wines. The tenders hailed their prices.

Sandy and his benefactor, Dr. John Osborn, the head of the orphanage, stepped into the scene. The doctor was a tall, thin man. He wore an old top hat. His wrinkled brow showed his age. A long, bulbous nose perched in the middle of his sallow, triangular face. His alert, brown eyes fell upon the clipper, Falcon.

"Well, there she is, Sandy. A full-rigged ship with royals high," he declared.

Sandy's mouth dropped open as he took a sharp intake of breath. His eyes feasted upon the sleek lines and fresh paint of the clipper before him. "She's a beauty!" he exclaimed and raced forward for a closer look.

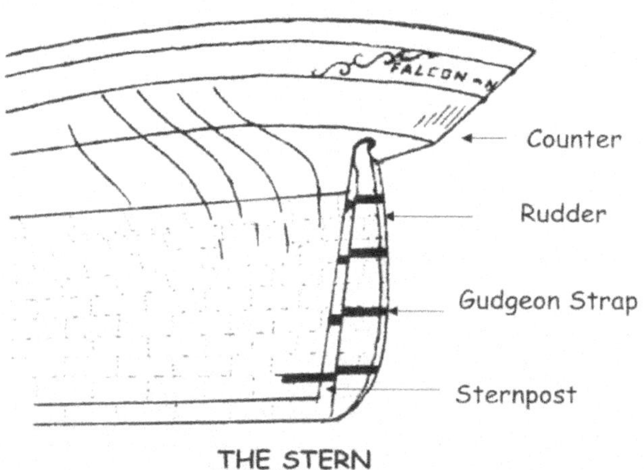

THE STERN

The Falcon was indeed a shapely maiden. Sandy noted that her stern was rounder than any other that he had seen. Its counter sloped long to the sternpost. This in turn slanted inwards as it dropped below the water line. The rudder arched aft being horizontally striped by the gudgeon straps. White scroll picked out her stern carvings and her name. Reflected rays of sunlight flickered across the black paint and the copper plating as Sandy moved along her port side. A white line beneath her bulwarks traced her sheer. It was broken only by the chain-plates under her double channels.

Seventy strides found the boy gloating over her bow. Her sides hollowed and narrowed along to the sharp, concave stem that reached upwards and forwards to the flying white falcon that was her figurehead. Bright varnish emboldened the dark grain of her bowsprit and jibboom as they stretched out to grasp the jib stays. The martingale thrust itself

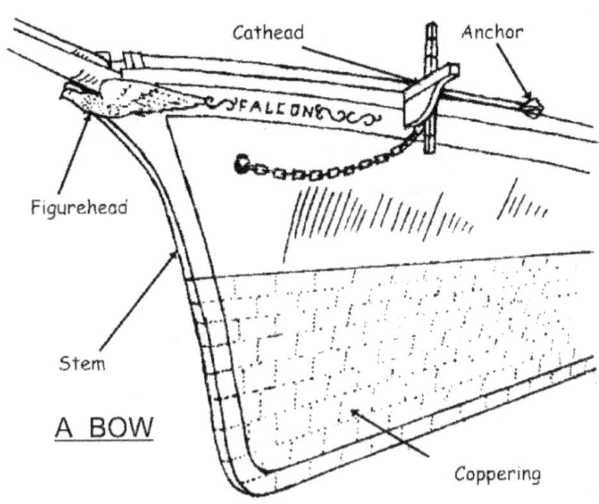

downward to spread the ropes and chains. White scrolled mouldings graced her cheeks and bore her name. A huge chain fell across to her anchor that was lashed to the side at the end of the cathead. Trying to view her tall masts, Sandy walked backwards, straight into the hands of the patient doctor.

"I'm glad you've chosen to go to sea, lad," he said. "It's a hard life. Dangerous too. But you look, listen and learn, and you'll be richly rewarded."

Sandy nodded. Then hearing a call, he turned his head. There behind a barrel leaned a stocky man appealing to a group of sailors who loitered nearby. He cried out poetically.

<blockquote>
"Come along now, lads.
The land is not for ye.
Sign aboard clipper Falcon,
And get ye gone to sea."
</blockquote>

A shabby man stepped forward. "Who's her skipper, Greybeard?" he asked loudly.

"Finest captain ever sailed the rough and calmer. None other than Captain Matthew Palmer," came the reply.

The seaman stepped back proclaiming, "I've heard o' him. They say he be record mad and drives his men like slaves. 'Sides, I hear that Falcon be a doomed ship - launched with Adam's Ale. Poor show that. I've a mind to find another ship, thank 'e."

He turned to his companions. They nodded their agreement. The gang moved off. The aproned man with the grey beard shrugged his shoulders and resumed his call.

> "Come along, m'lads,
> Get ye gone to sea.
> Be a well paid hand on clipper Falcon
> With tall masts three."

Osborn's gaze met that of Sandy. 'Greybeard' spotted them and beckoned him, "Come now, lad. No need to look so sad."

Sandy looked from the musterer to the clipper and then to the doctor. "I'm scared, doctor," he uttered.

"It's only to be expected, Sandy," comforted the doctor. "Every worthwhile step in life is hard until it's taken. You have cleared all your business. Captain Palmer has accepted responsibility for you. He's signed the necessary papers. Now, step forward with a lion's heart."

Having proved the wisdom of the doctor's advice in the past, the youth approached the old salt whose face brightened into a toothless smile.

> "Fine to see thee, lad.
> Wise thou be.
> Now be so good
> T'give thy name to me."

"Sandy Scott, sir. That's my name," informed the boy.

The experienced sailor scribbled Sandy's name into a large book. "Ah, the captain mentioned 'e. A grand title. No doubt bound for fame," he added. Then, giving the lad the pen, he pointed to a space on the page. "Sign here, m'boy. Then, say thy farewells and climb the plank when thou hears the bell."

Many thoughts raced through Sandy's mind as he signed. He put down the pen and turned to the doctor who offered him the small canvas bag containing all his belongings. Sandy took it. John Osborn then drew his own Bible from his coat pocket.

"I'd like you to have this Sandy," he said.

"But, Doctor, it's your own Bible!" resisted the boy.

"Take it, Sandy. It's not only a ship that needs a pilot when in hazardous waters."

Overwhelmed, Sandy dropped his bag and flung his arms round the tall man. Tears welled up into his eyes as he embraced the man who had been a father to him.

"Thank you. Thank you for all that you've done for me," he sobbed.

John Osborn swallowed hard and fought back his own tears. Sandy Scott had, in turn, been like a son to him.

Falcon's bell rang. The embrace was broken. The doctor held the boy at arm's length. His forefinger flicked away the lad's tears.

"Take your leave now, Sandy," he smiled, again offering the book. Sandy reluctantly took it and, bending, put it into his bag.

"I'll take care of it, Doctor John," he promised.

"God go with you, lad."

Sandy lifted the holdall. They vigorously shook hands and the boy turned to the clipper. Neither of them noticed the rugged sailor who had been casting sly glances towards them; the seaman who went to the old sea dog and signed on; the man who followed them to the gangplank.

Sharply, an order rapped out, "NEW HANDS ON DECK. NO TIME TO WASTE!"

Sandy looked up to see a stocky seaman whose dark cap sat back upon a mop of black hair. His eyebrows were equally as thick and met above a snub nose. A full beard matted his chin and cheeks. His steel-grey eyes met those of the boy who, in haste, stumbled and fell headlong to the deck. The mate, for that's who he was, came and towered above him. Sandy lifted up his head to see a knotted rope dangling before his eyes. "You, boy," he hissed through clenched teeth, "look sharp now, or my rope's end you'll taste."

However, caring hands took hold of the boy's shoulders and lifted him. The mate strode away leaving Sandy in the hands of the grey-bearded enlister.

"Who's that monster?" asked the teenager. The rescuer's finger darted to his lips.

"Ssh, now, lad. That there's the first mate. Quick! Get thou into line."

The old hand ushered Sandy to the end of the line of new crewmen gathered upon the main deck. The first mate stepped back to sit against the bulwarks. His knotted rope regularly slapped into his left palm as he scrutinised the remnants before him. He was not pleased. They were mostly dregs of humanity. They included drunkards who were frail in body. Their eyes bulged from reddened sockets. Then there were the ruffians just hired from New York's jailhouse. These were scarred and filthy. Others looked sick and ailing.

"Call themselves seamen," thought the officer. "Looks like we've hired a keg of trouble for this trip." Spotting the Captain, he stood and barked, "STAND TALL! Captain's approaching." The line lifted, but not without a groan.

Matthew Palmer was dressed in a faded three-piece suit. It was dark and baggy. "Is this the last lot of crew, Douglas?" he asked the mate.

"Aye, Sir. Sixteen of the most miserable scum I've ever set me eyes upon. Another two are sleeping it off in the hold."

"What about those?" asked the captain as he pointed to a good number of men on the windlass and foredeck. They were raising the starboard anchor.

"I've sailed with many of those before, captain. They know what they're about and can be trusted," assured the mate.

Palmer nodded. He turned to the line. Scorn lifted the left side of his upper lip. "Listen to me!" he boomed. "I've sailed with hundreds of men calling themselves seamen, but not one bunch poorer than you are."

The line shuffled uncomfortably.

"All you have on your puny minds is the gold of California."

Heads lifted. He was right.

"But get this clear - this is my ship, and you'll jump to my chorus until we reach the Golden Gate."

Several of the men grunted. Others looked disapprovingly.

"When we get out of dock every inch of sail will be raised and woe betide any man who cuts them down."

The men growled their exclamations. One or two stepped forward threateningly then retreated as the captain bellowed, "THEY'LL STAY UP EVEN IF I HAVE TO PADLOCK THEM UP! And, before we go any further, I want every bag and chest emptied here and now. JUMP TO IT!"

Unwillingly, the men turned out their bags. An assortment of clothes, bottles and weapons temporarily littered the deck. Palmer turned to the old salt who had helped Sandy.

"Sail-maker, collect every whisky bottle and knuckle-duster, knife and pistol and store them in my cabin."

Several men protested. One skinny wretch attacked the sail-maker as he was taking a whisky bottle from among his belongings. The knot of the mate's rope burned his ear and he returned to line. Quickly, 'Greybeard' hunted through the litter and dumped the offensive goods into a canvas bag. Douglas, the mate, then frisked the men's belts and pockets for further stocks. He found one knife and two pistols. They followed the others.

"Now," resumed the captain, "if any of you have a disagreement you can settle it with bare knuckles. Douglas, berth the men and then lick them into shape. Archie, you take care of the lad and show him the ropes."

"Right, my lovelies, load your bags," ordered the mate. The motley crew did so. "Now, follow me."

As the men were led away, Matthew Palmer shook his head before returning to his chartroom where the pilot was waiting for him. "You've a rum lot there, captain," he said. "What with a rabble for a crew, and with the noose of superstition hanging over your yards, you'll be fortunate to reach the Horn, let alone the Golden Gate."

"I respect your opinion, Bill," replied Palmer, "but I ain't lost a ship yet, and I don't intend losing this one."

The Captain spread the chart on the table, and the two veterans once again ran their fingers through the local channels.

Chapter 4
"A wise man will hear, and will increase learning" Proverbs 1:5.

Having stowed their gear, the recruits were now on deck helping to finish stowing a few items of remaining cargo under the scrutiny of the first mate.

The ship was full of mining tools and machinery, coal, iron, cast steel, wagon parts, powder, carpets, clothing, glass items, cutlery, stationery and gourmet foodstuffs along with brandy and whiskey. It even included three piano-fortes. Bales of cotton duck were added last in order to fill in the odd spaces left in the hold. All had been placed as carefully as possible so as to balance the ship across her beam and along her hull.

The twenty passengers who came from Massachusetts and New York were all checked in and had been shown to their quarters. Soon the tide would be in their favour and they would be steered out of harbour by the pilot.

Sandy stood peering at the maze of rigging silhouetted against the sky. The puzzled expression on his face showed his bewilderment. A well-worn hand fell gently upon his shoulder. He had been joined by the sail-maker.

"Fear not, lad," he reassured. "Thou'lt soon know the Falcon inside out."

"But how? There seems to be so much - so many…!"

"Look thou," interrupted the old salt, "Just think wide at first and thou'lt soon understand. Come with me."

Sandy was led to the main hatch. There the sailor lifted a folded sheet of canvas from the pocket of his apron. He carefully opened it, and stretched it over the top of the hatch. Sandy gulped. There, lying before him was a detailed picture of the Falcon. The marvel was that every line was stitched. The old man's eyes twinkled.

"Dost thou like it?" he asked. Sandy was speechless. "Did every stitch myself," added the proud sail-maker. Sandy's finger raced along the lines.

"I've never seen its like," burst from his lips. "It's beautifully worked."

The sailor's face wrinkled into a wide grin. "Aye, I'm proud of this, I must declare. Now, let's start to educate thee. I reckon that the best way t'learn facts is by singing them. Oh, by the way, thou canst call me Archie."

"Archie," repeated the boy. It fitted the little man to a tee.

Archie stood as straight as a poker. "Listen to this," he instructed. He cleared his throat and sang,

> "There be the mizzen, main and foremast,
> Made from timber, built to last.
> Each of these be cut in three,
> Joined at top and high crosstree."

He stopped, prodded Sandy, and said, "Thy turn, lad. Sing with me."

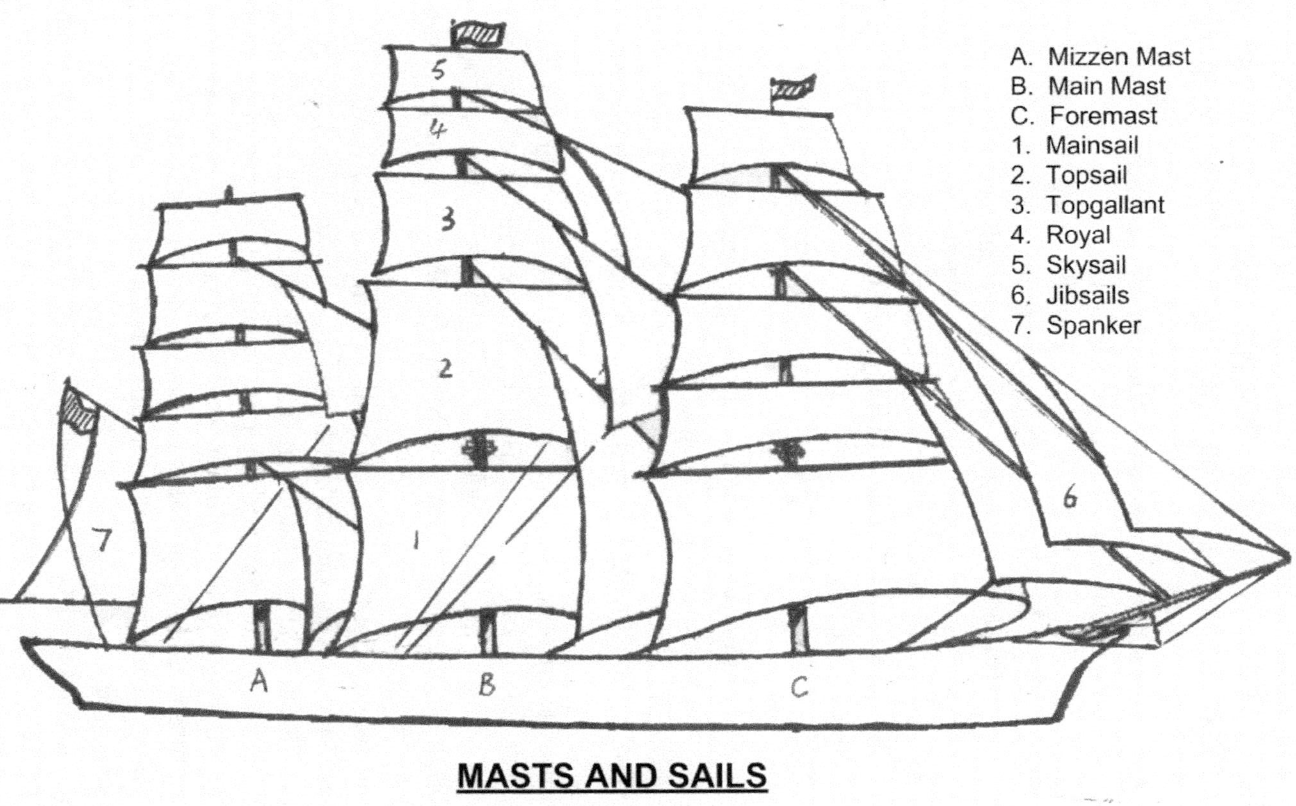

MASTS AND SAILS

Reluctantly, Sandy sang along with Archie. He was soon word perfect. Then his teacher asked to be taken to each mast in turn. The teenager obeyed. The song echoed in his mind as he pointed out the masts and named them. He had mastered his first lesson. The tar praised the boy as they returned to the main hatch.

"How many sails across each mast?" questioned the teacher.

Sandy counted them quickly. "Five," he replied.

"Right again, lad. Thou'rt learning fast," complimented the sail-maker. Immediately, he cleared his throat and sang another verse.

> "There be mainsail, topsail and t'gallant,
> Made from cotton - cut to slant.
> Royal and skysail above them fly,
> Tied to yards and hanging high."

Archie nodded to Sandy.

"I don't think that I can remember all those," he said as he shook his head.

"Never fear," comforted his teacher. "I'll sing a line, and then thou canst sing it. We'll soon learn it, so don't thou fret."

Their voices filled the air. Even the roughest of the crew grinned their appreciation of Archie's teaching methods. Soon Sandy had two lessons under his belt.

Meanwhile, the crew had been active in casting off and the ship had been safely towed down the East River to Batter Point where the tow was cast off. The ebb tides being right, the crew began to set the sails. The south-westerly breezes soon drove the clipper down to Sandy Hook where the pilot was discharged.

It was not long before the ship was well out into the North Atlantic. Astern, Long Island was a shortening, black slug. To starboard, the coastline of New Jersey loomed large and green. The sails of the Falcon continued to be unfurled one after the other and she cut through the waves more swiftly. The Atlantic winds pushed the clipper southwards under her bellying sails and creaking masts. Cold spray rained upon the deck as she ran with the tail end of the Labrador Current. Sandy felt alive as the breeze played with his hair - alive and free.

Archie noticed the boy's momentarily glazed eyes. He knew what the youth was thinking. He also knew that there were much harder lessons to come. The sailor's lot was a bitter one.

"How's the boy doing, Archie?" The voice of the captain broke in on their daydreaming.

"He's a good un, Captain Palmer. He has a good mem'ry and a good voice," replied the sail-maker.

"Aye. I heard yer singing. A better way of learning than in my day," said the captain.

"Didst thou learn by the rope then, sir?" asked Archie.

"That I did, Archie. I had a cruel taskmaster," puffed the master. The captain spotted Douglas. Taking his pipe from his tobacco stained teeth, he called, "Douglas, here if you will."

The first mate spun around and strode across to the captain. "Sir?" he asked.

"Douglas, you and Archie are the most responsible of my crew. Report to the chart room and we'll go over our proposed route." With that he headed off to his quarters. Archie wondered what to do with Sandy. However, the captain stopped and shouted, "You'd best bring the boy. He may as well know what a chart's about."

Sandy's face brightened. They followed the skipper to the chart room. There they approached a large table laden with maps. They leaned over to look at the map on top of the pile.

"I intend to hug the coast down to Virginia Beach and take advantage of the day breezes," began Palmer. "If we swing further east to use the westerly winds we'll have to fight the Gulf Stream, and there's the danger of weed in

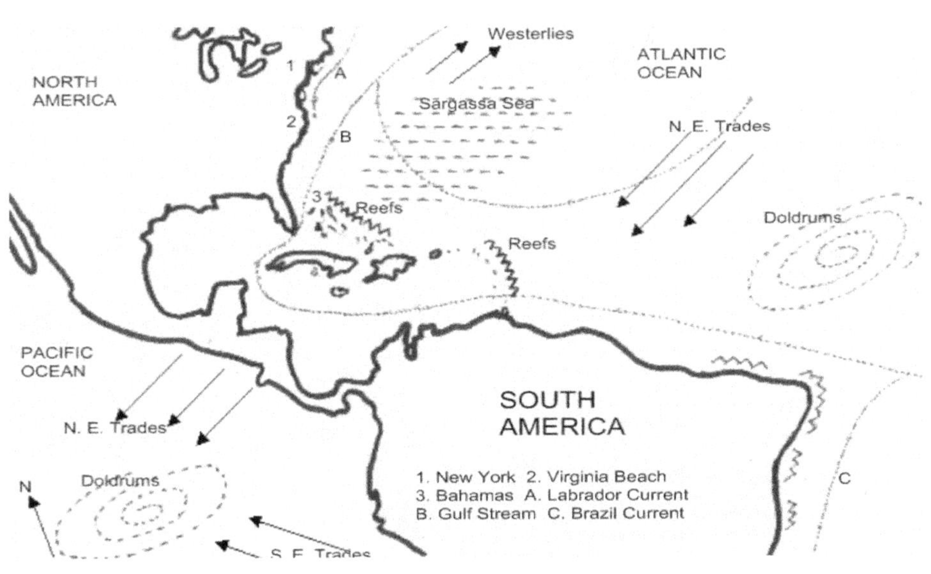

the Sargassa Sea fouling the rudder. From Virginia, we'll swing Southeast. This should avoid any hurricanes from the Caribbean and allow us to pick up the Northeast Trades. Hopefully, they'll drive us to the eastern tip of Brazil. Any questions so far?"

Archie and the mate looked at one another. Then Jim Douglas spoke up. "Forgive me, sir, but if we aren't careful we could hit the coral reefs."

"Coral reefs, mate?" queried the captain, raising his eyebrows. "There are no coral reefs marked on this chart."

Archie leaned further forward. "Sorry, sir, but there are reefs," he affirmed.

Matthew Palmer offered him a pen. "Here, Archie. Mark them in," he directed. Archie took the dipped pen from the captain. He marked a number of zigzagging lines east of the Bahamas and east of the West Indies down to Trinidad. He paused. "And here, Archie," prompted the mate pointing to the eastern tip of Brazil. Archie added more lines, and then he returned the pen.

"Gentlemen," said the captain as he slid the chart to one side, "let's see how accurate your lines are." Underneath the first chart lay an almost identical one. However, marked on it were the same coral reefs that Archie had just drawn, and in the same positions. Archie and Jim realised that their captain had been testing them. They felt uncomfortable.

"I'm sorry that I had to try you out in that way," apologised the captain as he moved closer to the two men. "Now I know that I may leave the ship in the hands of two reliable men." He put a hand on the shoulder of each man. "Well done," he said.

He then moved to a cabinet. As he opened its door the sailors saw three small glasses. Each glass contained a tot of rum. Again the eyes of Jim and Archie met. The captain had obviously anticipated their ability. Palmer gave each man a glass and, with a toast of a safe voyage, they sipped the drink. It was good.

The captain then asked Douglas about the latest recruits. The first mate reported to the captain that the new men were weak and slow at their work, but that all but one had sailed before. He also spoke of the two men who were supposed drunk.

Apparently, they had some kind of sickness. Palmer then dismissed the men and the apprentice. The seamen put their empty glasses on the table and left with an honourable respect for their captain.

Sandy didn't know what to think. As he had stared at the charts he had become hot. Now sweat was pouring down his neck. His head was thumping madly. He felt strangely light and a queasy feeling filled his abdomen. He reached the starboard bulwarks in the nick of time.

Chapter 5
"Enter not into the path of the wicked" Proverbs 4:4.

When the sail-room of a clipper is turned into a sick bay the crew know that something is seriously wrong. For eighteen days, the Falcon had sliced through the waves. Favourable winds had breathed into her sails. The pallor of the men had adopted a healthy, red glow, and, although they had groaned under the work load of trimming and sailing the ship, they had sung well to the sound of the banjo when at their ease. Broken fingernails blistered palms and, at times, bleeding fingers had etched Sandy's lessons into his mind. The apprentice was very tired, but, even so, found the life thrilling.

Now, at 6 am on Tuesday, 5th April 1850, a hush hovered over the ship. The whisper, "She was launched with a bottle of water, you know," slid about the anxious watch.

All eyes glanced nervously at the companion way that led down to the sick bay because Ned 'Beans' Perkins, the acting ship's doctor, had summoned the captain and first mate to see the two sick men below. There, Ned carefully mopped the brows of the two sweating men. They looked half-dead. He then scrubbed his hands with soap in a bucket of water, rose up, took a clean towel and, silently, dried them. Turning to the captain, he solemnly declared, "These men have typhoid."

Matt Palmer was unmoved. He asked calmly, "Are you sure?" The doctor met Palmer's gaze with cold, blue eyes. At that moment one of his patients clutched his stomach and stiffened with the agony.

"Positive," the doctor affirmed. "I should have spotted it earlier. They've been feverish since they came aboard. Then there was the diarrhoea. A real mess it was. And look there," he added, pointing to the face of the nearest man.

"The small red spots?" queried the mate. "Yes," said Ned. "Those red spots, delirium and the pains all signal typhoid. By my reckoning they'll live or die in the next few hours."

"How d'you think they came by it?" asked Palmer.

"Bad water or bad food in New York, I guess," replied Ned.

"So it isn't caused by something on board?"

"No," answered Ned. "Pete said that they've had those spots for over a week. They usually show ten days after the start of the fever, if they get 'em at all. Those men must have contracted the disease just before they signed on.

"Thanks, Ned," returned the captain. "Oh, by the way, it's contagious ain't it?" It was a question to which he knew the answer. He didn't know why he had asked it.

"Yes, skipper. You just keep the men away from these two and make sure the ship's cook is informed. He'll make sure that the food's well and truly cooked. You'd better have the water boiled just to be sure. Finally, make sure the men get their hands clean, especially before eating."

The skipper nodded, nudged the mate and went up onto the deck. Knowing that all eyes peered at him he spoke quietly to the mate. "Douglas, get all the men out of their bunks. Muster them, the watch and the passengers on the main deck. I'll be along shortly."

The mate went about his duty. The captain paused and took out his pipe. He lit it. As he puffed, he wondered how he should break the news to his men. Sailors panic easily. One wrong word could lead to a mutiny. Palmer decided that he must be prepared. Quickly he slipped down to his cabin and unlocked the bottom drawer of his desk. He lifted out a pistol. He loaded its empty chambers using bullets from a box nearby and pushed it into his pocket. His hand clenched the weapon as he stepped aloft. Swift strides brought him to his audience. Silence and anticipation met him.

"Men," he began, "as many of you know, we have two men in the sick bay. They have typhoid fever."

"Typhoid!" they gasped as one man.

Palmer raised his left hand. They quietened.

"Doc says that there's nothing to fear provided you listen, and listen well. Firstly, those men had the fever when they came aboard, so it's unlikely that our food or water is contaminated. But, just in case, all the water will be boiled and all the vegetables well cooked. Secondly, every man will wash

well, 'specially after using the toilet. Last of all, no person, except those Doc says, are to visit those sick men."

Ahab Jackson pushed forward. Palmer's right hand tightened on the handle of the concealed gun. "Captain," scowled Jackson, "I've seen typhoid fever sweep through a ship afore - killed eighteen men before the cap'n."

Several men supported his claim. They had also met with typhoid.

"I say that we drop those typhoids at the nearest port," suggested the seaman. Many of the crew voiced their agreement. Matthew Palmer stepped up to face the rebel squarely.

"Step back, mister," he ordered. "Those men are my responsibility. They're in good hands. We will go on."

Jackson champed his teeth and momentarily stood his ground. Hate filled his eyes. He then retreated.

"Record mad! We've got a cap'n who's record mad!" he declared.

Matthew Palmer swung round.

"Dismiss the men, Douglas," he snapped.

"Aye, sir," said the mate. As the captain stamped to his quarters, Douglas thundered, "Remember what's been said. Now get back to work!"

The crowd dispersed noisily. Back in his quarters Captain Palmer was a worried man.

"Maybe I shouldn't have been so hard on Jackson," he thought. "I'd only lose a day or two by going into port. But then again, Ned reckons the next few hours will be decisive. I think I've done right. What I need is a diversion. Something for the men to think on - other than death!"

The skipper thought hard and long. Then he remembered the Falcon's position. Excited, he raced to his charts and checked his latitude.

"That's it!" he exclaimed, "The Line! We cross the Equator today. What better a diversion!" Soon the clipper was bubbling with the news that the "Crossing of the Line" ceremony would be held that afternoon.

Upon hearing the news, Ahab Jackson gathered several of his cronies behind the deckhouse. Sandy sat on the main hatch nearby practising the skill of splicing a rope. He was also speculating as to which of the crew had twice ransacked his belongings. Once he could understand; but twice, and with nothing taken, he could not. He had considered telling the mate, but he had no proof of it ever happening. The boy shuddered. Glancing up from his labours, he spied the group of ruffians clustered around the rebellious seaman. The loud whispers soared through the still air. Ahab's mood was black.

"Right, lads," he began. "The way I sees it is this - we want t'get t'California for the last o' the gold, but we wants t'get there healthy."

"Aye, s'right," agreed his chums.

"Well, I got a plan. It means takin' over the ship and stickin' the cap'n and chief officers in irons. Then we throw them two typhoids t'the sharks. You with me so far?"

"Down the line, Ahab," said one.

"Aye, we shouldn't have much bother from this lot," observed the other.

Ahab spoke more confidently, "Some time this aft'noon we'll be crossin' the line. While the crew's funnin', we'll take the ship. You, Jake, take the mate with 'Arry. Jesse, you should be able to manage the sail-maker. I'll take the cap'n. Them're the main uns. The rest o' you let the other discontents know. Then get t'makin' 'ats so's you can get behind the usual courtiers at the ceremony." The group buzzed with excitement.

"What'll be the sign then, Ahab?" asked the tiny Patch. Ahab's hand stroked his chin.

"Mmm. 'S a good point, Patch. Look. When I be behind the cap'n you get set. Then, when I waves me 'at, like this," he lifted his hat and twirled it overhead, "let 'em 'ave it."

"What about weapons, Ahab?" questioned Billy.

"Look around, man. There be plenty o' belayin' pins on the rails. Use 'em like clubs. 'Sides, 'Arry and Jake have knives." The two named men cautiously raised their trouser legs to reveal dark hilts protruding from the tops of their boots.

"I've a pistol," reassured Ahab. "Remember the signal. Then let 'em 'ave it." Overtaken with the joy of the moment Ahab laughed loudly.

Sandy, whose ears had been pricked up anyway, sat bolt upright. The screeching laugh of Ahab Jackson was unique. It was the laugh of Jack Crocker's murderer. Sandy's mind flashed into the past. The wide brimmed hat that hung from Jackson's shoulders, and the chequered bandanna that circled his throat verified the fact. The boy then realised who had ransacked his bag. "But why?" he thought. All that the apprentice had as a memento of that night was a torn piece of paper. His hand raced to the purse slung from his belt. The paper was still there.

Sandy's thoughts were interrupted by the voice of the tireless mate who had also heard the laugh.

"Break it up, you men! You're blockin' the deck. And you two..." he shouted, pointing at two of Ahab's pals, "get back to work, you lazy lubbers!"

Fists clenched and teeth gritted. The conspirators would have attacked then had it not been for their leader's whisper, "Not now lads. Later."

Grins stretched their lips as they anticipated the fun that they would have that afternoon. They dispersed. Jim Douglas frowned as, arms akimbo, he watched them leave. Then, spotting Sandy, he walked to the hatch. His frown melted into a smile.

"Well, lad, how's it goin'?"

"It's a bit hard," answered the youth. "My fingers are so sore and they're cramping a little."

The mate nodded. The feeling was well known to him.

"Time'll teach you, lad. And it'll harden those hands, don't you fear."

He turned to go. Sandy grabbed his wrist. Swivelling, the mate raised his rope. It stayed high.

"Mr. Douglas," whispered Sandy urgently, "Will you take me to see the captain?"

Jim stowed his rope in his belt.

"Why, lad? 'Re you ailing?"

"No. You've got a murderer on board, and he's planning a mutiny."

Douglas stared into the lad's face. It was sincere. Then he thought about the rapscallions who had just departed. He said, "Having seen that lot, I can well believe you. Come on, boy, let's pay the captain a visit."

Chapter 6
"Who so diggeth a pit shall fall therein" Proverbs 26:27.

The next morning saw the winds drop to a flutter as the Falcon skirted the western edge of the Doldrums. The sun blazed through the skylight into the captain's quarters to highlight the wet ink which marked an additional entry in the ship's log:

'Mid-morning: Things are worsening. As if the news of two men having typhoid wasn't enough, now the crew is divided. A group is planning to mutiny. Jim Douglas (first mate) and Sandy Scott (apprentice) reported to me at 7 am, Scott had overheard Ahab Jackson, Sid 'Patch' Anderson, and several other men, planning to take over the ship and to ditch the two sick men into the sea. Scott also suspects that Jackson is wanted for murder back in New York. The boy has given to me part of a document. It seems to be part of a land-claim form and bears the signature of Jack Crocker. Should Jackson have the other half of this paper, it would confirm Scott's suspicions. Plans to thwart the mutiny have been made. However, if anything should go wrong, this may be my last entry.
Matthew Palmer (Captain).'

As soon as the ink had dried, Palmer closed the book and hid it on top of his cabinet. He then went up to the main deck, lit his pipe and surveyed the ship as if nothing was amiss. The carpenter (who worked hard on any voyage) was making studdingsail yards. Sandy was painting over the brass on the rails to save polishing them during the voyage. Archie was sewing extra skysails, as they were frequently lost in a sudden squall. Most of the watch was busy aloft with the maintenance of the masts and rigging, while the resting men set their hands to prepare for the 'Crossing of the Line' ritual. Yet, among that hustle and bustle, Palmer could see his plan forming.

Sandy had soon finished. He was hot and bothered (and that not only because of the intense tropical heat). Throughout the morning he had been conscious of more eyes than ever before. He had even seen thumbs jerked his direction, and the men seemed to drop their voices when he passed by.

"It must be something to do with the mutiny," he sighed.

Douglas examined his work. "You've made a good job o' that rail lad. Wash the brush and stow the paint. Make sure you do that carefully. Many a fire has been caused aboard ships because of vapour escaping from tins of paint and varnish," he said. "Then take a break."

Sandy expressed his thanks and quickly obeyed. Having stowed the paint securely, the boy went back to the deck. He approached the busy sail-maker. "Hello, Sandy," greeted the little fellow. "Hast thou nought to do?

"No," replied the youth.

"Well, there's a hook and line. Wilt thou do some fishin'?" asked Archie.

Sandy ignored the question. "Archie, what *is* going on around here?" he asked abruptly.

The sail-maker stopped working. "Hast thou not been told, lad?"

"No."

"But surely thou know'st that we cross the line today?"

Sandy's face screwed up a little. "What is 'crossing the line'?" he asked.

"That's simple. The line is the Equator. We cross it today," answered the tar as nonchalantly as possible.

"I know that it's the Equator. What I really want to know is why some of the men are making hats and things. And what happens at this ceremony thing?"

Archie thought carefully before replying. "Well, lad, because the Doldrums is a miserable place for sailors we have a bit of actin'. The crew are just making silly costumes."

Sandy detected a glint in the eye of his friend and the lump in his right cheek filled by a rolling tongue. Archie turned back to his work. The boy knew that all had not been told.

"Archie.... Can I join in? Am I allowed to make a costume and act?"

The craftsman lifted his head. Sandy saw that toothless grin again. "Well,

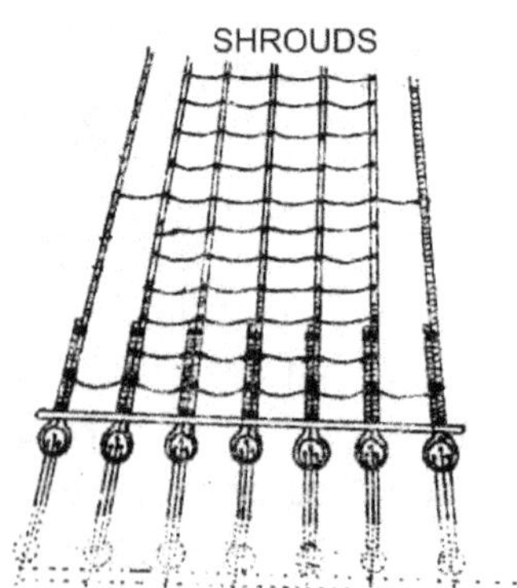

apprentices usually get the star part," whispered the old salt, "but with the mutiny and all, thou art best left out of it."

The youth frowned as a bell sounded. Most of the seamen scurried below. Sandy sat quietly reflecting upon the day's events. Many of the passengers emerged from their quarters in order to see the show. A few sailors lounged along the deck, and the captain sat on a barrel by the side of the deckhouse.

Suddenly, the deckhouse door opened. A stocky seaman stepped out onto the deck. Upon his head was a painted saucepan. Pieces of string were tied in bows on his rough beard. Large curtain rings hung from his ears and nose. The oil on his skin shone from a blue shark tattooed on his bare chest. A short towel, belted at his waist, served as a loincloth. His legs were naked except for thick dark hairs. He carried a hand-bell that rang out as he leapt onto the port bulwarks and grasped the shrouds.

"Hear ye! Hear ye! Hear ye!" he cried. "The Doldrums are quiet, an' the sun's a' shining. Prepare for the king o' the seas. Make his court ready. Hear ye! Hear ye! Hear ye!"

As the herald scrambled down from his perch, other seamen with some amazing hat inventions, processed into the scene. Each carried a staff of sorts, and most were bared to the trunks.
Sandy moved forward with a smile on his lips. Never had he seen such an assortment of arms, legs and stomachs. The men formed two rows in front of the bulwarks and faced the deckhouse. Ahab Jackson's rebels wore brightly coloured cloth hats and stood behind the other courtiers who wore saucepans as theirs.

The herald then demanded, "Is the court ready?"

"The court of King Neptune is ready," replied the men.

The herald rang his bell. "Make way for King Neptune and his queen," he cried.

The audience and courtiers alike cackled with laughter as the king and queen emerged from the deckhouse. The crown of the king was a polished paint tin. It sat upon the head of a mop that was employed as a wig. This not only covered the head but veiled the face. The king's body was painted green. A piece of canvas covered his loins and a long flag served as a cloak. In his right hand he held a pitchfork to represent his sceptre.

At his left hand side walked his queen. A cardboard crown graced her hair that consisted of long strands of thin rope that dangled to the deck. She wore a long white tunic that was tied at the waist with a thicker rope. Her face was emboldened with huge, painted lips and gave her a clown-like appearance. Her bare arms and legs were covered with squirming black hairs. Her swollen hips rocked, and her belly bounced as she and the king majestically proceeded to their thrones.

The herald proclaimed, "Make way for Neptune, King of the Sea. Bow the knee."

Most of the courtiers bowed stiffly as the monarchs sat into deckchairs. A drummer rolled upon a large can. The herald again raised his voice, "Court is in session. Call the first offender."

Sandy was beginning to enjoy the show. A courtier stepped forward. "As clerk of this court, and by the authority of Neptune," he declared, "I call..." He lifted his standard and pointed to a longhaired seaman. "I call Jonathan Samson."

Samson's upper lip lifted and his brow creased. He did not know what was happening. Two courtiers raced forward, grabbed him fiercely by the arms and threw him down before King Neptune. The audience laughed loudly, but Sandy was uncertain.

"What is his crime?" requested the King. He looked at a sheet he had been given. "John Samson," he read, "on the day of the fourteenth of March, you did unlawfully catch a barracuda - a very tasty fish - do you plead guilty or not guilty?"

"Well I did catch a fish, but there ain't nothin' unlawful about that," replied the accused.

King Neptune stood. "Jonathan Samson," he boomed, "I am the judge of the sea. With what did you catch the fish?"

"Why, with a hook, line and bait of course." He was pressed. "Your Majesty."

Neptune's face scowled. He lowered his sceptre so that its points were only inches from Samson's head.

"Neptune's law declares that no man should fish with a hook and line," stated the king.

"But why not, your Majesty?" asked the seaman. "Because it makes fish lazy eaters," answered Neptune.

"Hear! Hear! It makes fish lazy eaters," echoed the courtiers.

"But that be ridiculous," said Samson. "What should I have used then, your Majesty?"

Neptune turned to his courtiers. "Court of King Neptune," he began, "tell this man of the land what he should fish with."

"A NEW FANGLED BASEBALL BAT!" they shouted.

"A baseball bat, your majesty!" exclaimed Samson.

King Neptune lifted his sceptre. The herald placed a black cloth on his crown. "Jonathan Samson, I find you guilty," pronounced Neptune who then turned to his wife. "Now wife, strength of my life, what sentence shall I impose?"

The queen stood, shook her stomach and, pointing to the guilty one, said, "Always it grieveth me to see a man with such handsome hair. So the judgement ought to be - a knife to shave his head bare."

"HAIRCUT!" exploded from the lips of the king.

The condemned man pleaded for his hair as the two attendants pinned him to the deck. Another of the king's retinue joined them brandishing a knife. As tufts of hair flew right, left and centre, the courtiers chimed in unison, "Samson has been given the chop."

As the captain moved forward for a closer look, Ahab Jackson slipped in behind him. Simultaneously, the renegade waved his hat and dug his pistol into Palmer's back.

Seeing Ahab's signal the mutineers went into action. A bucket was slotted over the head of Archie, and his arms were pulled behind his back and forced upwards. Jake bent low behind the mate and Harry shoved Douglas backwards. As he rolled onto Jake's back the latter straightened quickly and threw him far down the deck. Harry followed and, jamming a knee into his spine wrenched back his head. The mate shammed unconsciousness. Harry relaxed his grip. Meanwhile, the rebels behind the courtiers raised their belaying pins.

"One move and the captain's dead meat!" rasped Ahab. "We be takin' over the ship."

The passengers, surprised and frightened, moved away; but Matthew Palmer remained as cool as marble. There was a moment of silence. Palmer's lips came together to form a grin. Then they opened, shouting, "AHAB!"

The faithful among the crew ripped into action. Up from the barrel behind Ahab popped a seaman. His belaying pin crunched into Ahab's skull. The boots of Archie stamped down upon the bare feet of his attacker who released him and hopped backwards to the bulwarks. The third officer swung across the deck to smash hard into the little man's attacker. He was sent flying over the side. One of the passengers had the sense to throw him a float of cork tied to a rope. Back in the fray, Jim Douglas rammed back his elbow into Harry's shoulder and sent him reeling. Both men sprang up to face one another. Harry drew his knife and lunged at the mate. The latter grabbed the wrist of the mutineer with his left hand while his right fist felled his attacker with a single blow.

Jake, another rebel, was flattened by a seaman who dived on him from the top of the deckhouse. The courtiers turned. Belaying pins descended harmlessly upon their saucepan helmets that changed into maces as they swept them from their own heads onto those of the mutineers. The mutiny was thwarted in less than a minute.

"CLAP 'EM IN IRONS!" roared Palmer, "AND STOW 'EM WITH THE REST OF THE RATS!"

The deck was soon cleared of the assailants. The captain ordered that the sailor who went overboard should be dragged along behind for a while. He then urged the passengers and crew to take their places in order that the ceremony be continued.

Sandy was smiling when he went across to congratulate the captain. "Your plan worked a treat, sir."

"Aye Sandy. So far that is," puffed the skipper.

"You mean there's more, sir?" asked the boy.

"There's part o' this plan that thou knowest not, lad," interrupted Archie.

"What's that?" queried the youth. The answer came from another quarter. "Call Sandy Scott," bawled the clerk of the court.

Before Sandy could say, "Davy Jones", the sail-maker and captain had whisked him away to face King Neptune.

"'Thou didst want to act, lad," jibed Archie. "Now's thy chance."

The king loomed over the lad. "Sandy Scott, you're charged with sewing a sail with a needle instead of using a fishbone. How do you plead?"

The youth thought quickly. He knew that this was really fun for the crew at his expense. He also knew that there would be no escape. He decided to enter into the spirit of the thing - and act he would.

"Most honourable Neptune, King of the Sea," he flattered, "I must, in the presence of your great knowledge, admit my guilt in this matter. But things are not as they seem. With your Majesty's permission I will give my defence."

The King was caught off-guard. He frowned. His "wife" rose up and pushed him to one side. "The boy has admitted his guilt. There will be no defence," she declared. The crowd and courtiers jeered.

King Neptune recovered his composure.

"There will be no defence " he affirmed. "Blight of my life, what is the sentence?

The herald again put the black cloth over Neptune's crown. The queen described the sentence:

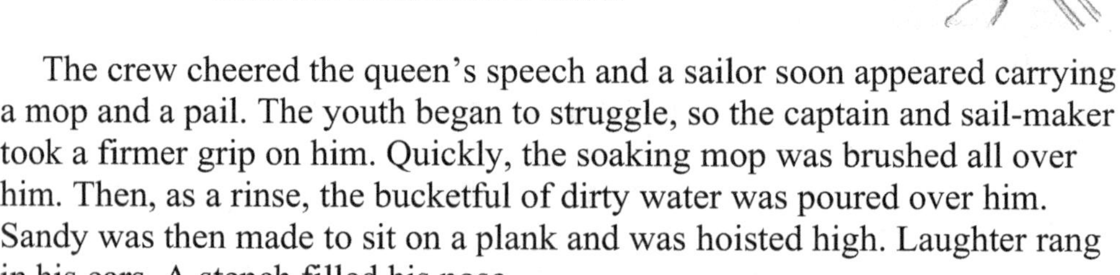

"A dirty boy 'tis sad to see
Upon a clipper bold,
So take a mop and scrub with glee
Until he shines like gold.
Then place the lad upon a plank,
With ropes and tackle tied,
And hoist him up to higher rank
Until his clothes have dried."

The crew cheered the queen's speech and a sailor soon appeared carrying a mop and a pail. The youth began to struggle, so the captain and sail-maker took a firmer grip on him. Quickly, the soaking mop was brushed all over him. Then, as a rinse, the bucketful of dirty water was poured over him. Sandy was then made to sit on a plank and was hoisted high. Laughter rang in his ears. A stench filled his nose.

"You and Samson can get your crossing the line sheet from my cabin this evening," shouted Matt Palmer. "Make sure you keep it somewhere safe though. You don't want this to happen again, do you?"

He turned and left. The crowd and court dispersed. Sandy sat, swinging on his perch, high above the deck.

Chapter 7
"Faithful are the wounds of a friend" Proverbs 27:6.

The day after his baptism, Sandy witnessed his first burial at sea. One of the brothers with typhoid had died. The service was held on the port side of the main hatch. The body, sewn into a blanket, lay on a plank by an opening in the bulwarks. An American Ensign was draped over it. A few of the crew, with hats in their hands and in solemn mood, circled the corpse.

"Shanty man," said the captain.

A gaunt, balding sailor lifted his eyes to heaven and sang:

> "Safe home, safe home in port
> Rent cordage, shattered deck,
> Torn sails, provision short
> And only not a wreck:
> But, O, the joy upon the shore
> To tell our voyage - perils o'er."

Matthew Palmer then nodded to the sail-maker who stood holding an opened Bible.

"For the wages of sin is death," he read, "but the gift of God is eternal life through Jesus Christ our Lord."

The little man cleared his throat. His eyes moved from the cloth coffin and met those of the seamen. "Men," he began, "Death is a great preacher. Look ye to that there body. 'Tis the life that's missing. Where d'ye think it be? Well, I'll answer. It be either in glory on heaven's brightest shore with our Lord Jesus - where all be at rest, or it be drifting out in the torment of Hades - where the storms are always raging. The verse I read shows us that the reward for our sin is death. Aye, death in this life and a living death in the life to come. But look ye, there be a gift that God offers each of us - eternal life! Aye, each one can have it 'cause God's Son, who never sinned, took sin's wages for us. He died so that we can have eternal life instead of sufferin' the second death. T'get it, we must turn back to God's ways and put our hands in those of His Son. It be real, my friends. Don't forsake God's offer 'cause this...." (he pointed to the body), "this will happen to us sooner or later."

Archie nodded to the captain who lifted a small prayer book. "Let's pray," he said. Their heads dropped to their chests.

"Forasmuch as it hath pleased Almighty God of His mercy to take the soul of this seaman, we therefore commit this body to the deep, looking for the resurrection of the body, and the life of the world to come, through our Lord Jesus Christ. Amen."

The mate held the flag as the plank was lifted. The body slid quietly down the timber and dropped with a slight splash into the sea. Sandy was choking with questions. He remembered words read by the doctor at the orphanage: "And the sea gave up the dead which were in it, and Death and Hades gave up the dead which were in them: and they were judged according to their works."

Palmer's hand fell gently onto his shoulder. The two looked at one another. Not a word passed, but Sandy knew that he wasn't the only one affected by the short service.

The following day proved more exciting. A wandering albatross landed on the deck. It was a huge, shining white bird with black tips to its wings. The ship fell silent. Slowly, the hands on watch surrounded the creature as it sat upon its haunches. Suddenly, the bird rose to its feet and ran. The sailors stopped. The albatross lifted its long wings in an effort to take off, but one of them struck the foremast ropes and sent the fowl crashing to the deck. Roaring, the men pounced. Sandy was amazed. He had previously thought that to kill an albatross would bring bad luck to a ship. Yet here he was - watching his companions killing, plucking and skinning one of them.

"Don't look so sad, lad," said Archie. "The men make baccy pouches and purses with the skin. Then they make pretty coats with the feathers."

"But it seems so cruel!" exclaimed Sandy.   "Not as cruel as some sailors, lad," purred Archie. "They see them flying and catch them with baited hooks. This one suffered little pain."

The mate overheard. "It also gives me an excuse to get the deck scrubbed," he added. "The crew don't mind cleaning up their own mess."

Sandy turned to Douglas. "Does anything else like this happen?" he asked.

The first mate told him that they sometimes fished for sharks. They did this to avenge the deaths of seafarers who had entered their jaws.

"We lay a baited hook," informed the mate, "and when the shark has taken it, we heave the blighter alongside. Then we lower a noosed rope so that it falls about its tail. Up we haul it, and then kill and gut it. Sometimes we make walking sticks with its backbone. A few superstitious sailors might nail the tail to the jib-boom to bring fair winds."

Other lessons were not so easy. For two days solid the captain ordered that practice be gained in reefing and furling the heavy canvas. Sandy's first ascent of the shrouds took him to the 'top' just above the fore sail's yardarm.

The top offered a temporary island of safety. Jim Douglas joined him.

"Sandy Scott," he began, "when you go out on that yard make sure that your feet are dug well into the foot rope, and get your arms well over the timber."

He pointed to some small loops of rope attached to the jackstays. "Them loops are called 'beckets'. Slide one of your arms well into the one nearest you so that it's well up on your shoulder. It'll keep you safe. Lastly, if you get a bit dizzy, give me a shout. I'd rather have you alive than dead."

The youth nodded. Douglas positioned the boy close to the mast. Soon he was balancing on the quivering footrope with his body arched over the yardarm. The voice of the shanty man filled the air.

"To me, WAY,
And we'll FURL,
And we'll pay Paddy Doyle for his BOOTS!"

Sandy was sharp to notice that the seamen hauled and cried out together on the word "BOOTS!" But he was panting too much with nerves to join with the shouts. As he stretched and pulled, his body rose almost to an horizontal position. The breeze was cooler and harder aloft. It tried to toss the labourer from the yard.

Now and then, Sandy found himself looking down at the rocking deck. The feelings that he had experienced in the captain's quarters overtook him again. However, it was not until he was swayed by dizziness that he called to the mate. Douglas pulled him onto the top. "Easy there, boy," he comforted. Sandy shivered. "Been lookin' at the deck, have you? Not surprising that you're green then. Remember to concentrate on the sail, not what's under it."

The teenager swallowed. He didn't really know what difference it would make.

"Now, here's another lesson for you," continued the mate. "Look at those men out there." He nodded towards those furling the sail. "They 'ave to work out there as a team or in bad weather the wind will tear the sail from their grip and from the yard. Their work is harder because you're not there. Remember that."

Sandy was stung by the sharpness in the voice of the mate who stepped into the boy's place upon the spar. Finally, the canvas was stowed in bundled folds and lashed to the yard by gaskets. The seamen moved across to the other side. The apprentice clambered down to resume his place on the other side of the mast. The mate grinned at seeing the pluck of the lad, but remained close by.

The clew lines, leech lines, bunt lines and the chant of the shanty man played their part in raising the canvas while the men aloft beat it into place. The youngster went at it with all his might and found, to his satisfaction, that he was enjoying it. Once upon the deck, the bucko congratulated him for his bravado. Sandy blushed.

So they 'furled' and 'let out' the sails faster and faster. The men were soon grumbling. It seemed so pointless. However, day or night, the officers drove them on until they were satisfied that every man knew his work and did it well.

Another exercise took the place of furling - trimming the sails to the wind. This meant swinging the angle of the yardarms so that the sails caught as much wind as possible in order to drive the ship forwards. Almost all the crew on the watch was needed for the job. The ropes that controlled the swing of the yards were called braces. These led down to through blocks to the bulwarks where they were belayed.

Sandy learned that, to trim efficiently, the braces on the side near the wind must be eased out as the braces on the other side (leeward) were hauled in. Again teamwork was essential as it took several men to handle each rope.

Trimming the sails was needed in the Doldrums where the wind was fickle, or when tacking (setting a zig-zag course against the wind), particularly in a storm. It was for this reason that most of the experienced seamen argued that Palmer was preparing the crew for the rounding of Cape Horn, while others contended that he was only interested in speed and records.

The first mate knew that the captain's motives were two-fold. The first was to keep the men busy to avoid mischief. The second was to maintain their fitness in preparation for the rapidly worsening conditions. Jim Douglas had the last in mind as he started for the captain's quarters.

There, Captain Palmer drew slowly upon his pipe and watched the whirling blue clouds of smoke swim up to the skylight. The smell of burning tobacco comforted him. Contented, he leaned back into his chair. His body relaxed but his mind's eye flickered back fourteen years. He envisaged his quiet wife smiling at him as he dandled his baby son on his knee. His gaze flashed to the happy times that they had spent together on the beach, and then to the time… A knock at the door plunged him back into reality.

"Come in," he grunted.

Douglas pushed his head around the opening door. "You wanted to see me sir?"

"Ah, Jim. Yes. Come in."

The officer closed the door and approached the captain.

"Sit down," ordered the captain. The man obeyed.

"How d'you think the men are shapin'?" continued Palmer.

"I reckon they've done pretty well, sir. They've bin hard at it this past week. They know what's expected of 'em. An' they ain't grumbled too much. Quite surprised me, they 'ave."

"I'm surprised too, Jim. I never expected very much of that lot."

"They're ready as ever they'll be," Douglas declared.

"That's mostly due to you and the other officers. I've watched you driving them on. Well done."

"Thank you, sir," blushed the mate.

Palmer stood. "As a token of my thanks, I've asked Archie to prepare something special for you all at dinner tonight. Let them know, won't you?"

"Aye, sir," replied Jim. Then he continued, "Forgive me, sir, but are you expecting trouble?"

The captain looked solemnly into his first mate's eyes.

"Very perceptive," he began. "Jim, we've been blessed with some of the fairest weather I've ever met on this tack. Even with a weakish crew, we've made a fast passage so far. But I trust my nose. I smell trouble. So, in the next few days I want some of the men on each watch to go into the hold and doubly secure the cargo. If we do hit a big one, I don't want a sack or keg moving. Others can replace any caulking that softened and lifted in the heat of the tropics. Also, get the stores and water barrels covered with extra canvas, and make sure there's a good supply of each in the lifeboats. We'd best be ready for the worst."

"Aye, aye, sir."

Douglas left the cabin. Matt Palmer went to his bunk knowing that he must snatch sleep while the going was good.

Chapter 8
"A merry heart doeth good like a medicine; but…"

The S.E. Trades, which had stiffened considerably, and the favourable Brazil Current were spurring the Falcon to speeds which manifested themselves in the full sails and flying spray. Matt Palmer had ordered a careful monitoring of the clipper's speed since the Doldrums. Each watch had to 'heave the log' at least once, but now, with the ship slicing through

the choppy seas, the orders were modified to streaming the log every hour.

As Sandy stood at the stern rails, he held a large piece of wood and looked towards 'Old Sage', a gaunt, balding sailor, who served as shanty man and storyteller; hence this nickname. He was standing, legs apart, holding aloft a large reel of thin rope which looped across the deck to join onto Sandy's wood block. Jim Douglas stood nearby holding a sandglass.

"Ready?" barked the bucko.

"Aye," they called.

"Go!" he ordered as he inverted the minute glass. Sandy threw the timber into the sea and played out the surplus of the knotted line. Soon the bobbin was spinning freely. At every hundred feet, a knot bumped over the rail. Sandy called its number. The minute expired.

"Hold!" commanded the mate.

"Log held," replied Old Sage grasping the reel.

"Fifteen knots, Sandy?" queried the mate.

"Fifteen knots, it is, sir."

"We're near flying, mate," commented Old Sage.

"Aye, I'll take the good news to the skipper. You'd best haul her in."

"Aye, aye."

Douglas turned to his heels, Sandy tugged at the line and the shanty man sang as he span the reel.

> "When I first went to 'Frisco Bay,
> I went upon a spree,
> Me hard-earned cash,
> I spent it fast,
> Got drunk as drunk can be;

Before me money was all gone
Or settled some old score,
I made up me mind,
Was fully inclined,
I'd go to sea no more."
"I wouldn't mind learning that one, Sage," said the boy.
"Aye, it's a good song. You might as well learn it. We'll echo."
So the shanty man sang and was followed by Sandy. By the time the wooden block stumbled over the rails they were singing it in unison.
"Have you really meant to leave the sea?" questioned the youth.
"Aye, lad, that I have," came the sure reply.
"But why?" asked Sandy.
"It's such a fine life even though the works hard. At least you're free.'"
The veteran's eyes bulged and stared past Sandy to the sea astern.
"Look back there, lad. The sea's bin kind to us these past few weeks but let me tell you, it don't take much to turn her into a monster. Sometimes she dives on a ship like an eagle on a rabbit. Her green talons seeking to squeeze the life from you. But you'll see. You'll see."
Sandy frowned. The tar shouldered the bobbin and trundled across the deck. He secured it behind the companionway, glanced back to the boy and left.

The helmsman, who had overheard their conversation, called to Sandy. "He's right, lad," he said. "It don't take much to make a lady angry, but there's no wrath like that of the sea when she's upset, believe me."

At that moment, the bell signalled the end of the watch. The deckhouse door opened and contented, cheerful sailors rolled out. They were in festive

mood. Jamaica Rum, the captain's token of thanks, had been well received. Happy officers popped out of the nearby companionway. The captain followed them. Spotting Sandy he directed him to the galley.

The whole of the first dog watch funnelled into the cookhouse. John Samson was leaving with a bowl full of dishes, and Archie was humming a hymn tune as he laid the table. Sandy recognised it as the tune to the hymn "At the Name of Jesus". He had often sung it at the orphanage. The hands sat down and, smelling rum, prattled together in excited anticipation of a good meal and half a mug. Archie put the dishes between the batons on the table.

"Real beef!" cried the storyteller as he speared the steaming meat with his knife. Archie's ladle rapped his hand. "Ouch!"

"Steady there," said Archie. "For a meal such as this we'll give thanks to the Lord." The men didn't argue. They bowed their heads. Archie rattled off a short prayer which was punctuated with a sharp "'men" from the diners who then charged at the food.

"Stretch or starve, Sandy," called the sail-maker. That was all the encouragement he needed. He joined the affray. Soon the only sounds were those of cutlery on tin and chomping jaws. The meal was good and there was plenty of it. Most of the seamen showed their appreciation with explosive burps and sighs of satisfaction. Old Sage was more poetic. He recited his revised version of the "Salt Horse" chant.

> "Salt horse, salt horse, we're sure you know,
> That to the galley you did go
> But there the cook, with magic brief,
> Has stirred you round and made you beef,
> And we filled sailors sitting here
> Have eaten you without much fear.
> So to the cook we raise our cheer!"

"Hooray! Hooray!" shouted the crew as they applauded the skill of both cook and shanty man. A louder cheer met the arrival of Archie carrying the rum. However, when the sail-maker omitted to fill Sandy's mug there were impolite words of disapproval. After some persuasion, Archie half-filled his mug. All eyes were fixed upon the teenager as he took his first swig. He took too much. His throat burned and his eyes watered as he gulped it down. A fit of coughing followed. His fellows laughed and toasted at the sight. Sandy pushed the mug away. A sea of grasping hands surged forward to win it.

Archie patted the boy's back. He then retrieved Sandy's mug and filled it with water. "Drink this, lad," he offered. "It'll ease thy cough."

Sandy swallowed the water. It was soothing.

"Rum be a good medicine in small doses," informed the sail-maker. "Take too much though, and it'll kick thee like a mule."

The doctor had given him similar advice. His words ran through his mind: "Strong wine bites like a serpent."

An officer called Jacob Rawlinson renewed Sandy's interest in the proceedings. He invited the shanty man to tell them a tale. The rest expressed agreement. Old Sage hesitated but a moment.

"Strange were the tale that began one midnight of August, 'forty-seven, down Sydney harbour way," he commenced. "As the wind slapped the waves against the cliffs by the South Head signal station, Harry Warner's daughter stirred him with a scream that could've woke up Davy Jones his self. When he got to her, sweat were streamin' down her face, and her eyes bulged out like marbles. She were tremblin'.

"Dad," she sobbed. "Dad, there's a wreck out there. And, there's a woman on the rocks screamin' for help. Help her, dad! Help her! She's got a baby tied to her!"

The lass fainted. Old Harry made her comfortable and went upstairs to scan the horizon. The scene were fairly calm. He shrugged it off as a nightmare. But for the next two days the wind strengthened and whipped the sea into a fury. With tremendous force it crashed into and climbed the cliffs to somersault backwards in a spray of white. About four o'clock the watch-keeper sighted a clipper tacking outside the Harbour Gap. The white dragon forming her figurehead identified her as the 'Serpent'."

"Captain Laws knows how to handle that ship," he thought. "He'll keep her right." Warner hoisted a routine flag signal but received no reply. Presuming that the sailors were too busy handling the ship to be bothered with signals, he went for a coffee. The noise of the storm became overpowering as the evening wore on. Meanwhile, Captain Laws apparently decided to try for anchorage. He knew that his rivals weren't far behind, and he wanted the first load bonus. 'Sides he had a reputation to keep up. So the captain and helmsman shaped up a course according to the lights. Lookouts were ordered to the foc'stle."

"BREAKERS AHEAD! BREAKERS AHEAD!" were the cries twenty minutes later. The helmsman and skipper pulled down hard on that wheel; but too late! The Serpent plunged forward onto rocks that whipped out her bottom. Crew and passengers were swept to their doom as the sea roared across the decks and filled her hull. The hammerin' of the waves soon broke her up completely. 'Twas mornin' before the disaster were known. Broken spars, planks and canvas littered the sand. The crowds gathered on the cliff-top and shore. All hope of survivors waned until a young fellow cried out. He'd seen somethin' on one of the rocks."

"He's right," exclaimed a man with a telescope. "It's a woman... and she's got a baby with her." Little Janie Warner's dream had become a reality...."

The diners buzzed.

"And what's more," added Sage, "the Serpent was launched with a bottle of water." The silence that followed was broken by the ship's bell. It was time for the next watch.

Archie approached Sandy as the men departed. "Sandy, thou hast heard a good tale, but remember - that ship sank 'cause the captain made a mighty blunder. His pride and his greed pushed him into making a foolish decision. Them two things are worse than any superstition. Them's the things that bring disaster and sorrow. Think on that, lad. Think hard." The boy went about his duty. It seemed much colder now.

43

Chapter 9:
" Perfect love casteth out fear" John 4:18.

"LAND AHOY!"

The cry broke the monotony of slapping waves on the forty-fourth day out. The men raced to the forecastle, followed by the captain. There, on the horizon, was a long, shark-like silhouette. "Tierra del Fuego?" asked the mate.

"Near enough," replied the ship's master, "Staten Island. We'll let these bitter Westerlies bend the sails to the south east for a while before we turn the Cape."

The crewmen returned to their duties. They were well wrapped up. Those who had oilskins wore them. Others had made makeshift waterproofs by smearing old clothes with linseed oil. Archie had supplied Sandy with a patched set of his own oilskins. It was baggy, but kept the bitterly cold winds and freezing water at bay.

His jaw set firmly, Matt Palmer peered at the grey stratus clouds ahead of the Falcon. He recognised them as the warm sector of a depression, and, hence, rain or snow. He then spotted a wedge of white cumulus behind the stratus. This marked an approaching cold front and signalled stormy weather.

"Blast!" he uttered in a puff of vapour that hung in the wintry air. "Storm! And around the Horn too!" Palmer knew that the Southern Ocean raced freely around the globe in a band two thousand miles wide. But between Cape Horn and the Antarctic all that sea was bottlenecked into a six hundred mile gap. The results were high seas, surging currents and violent winds. A storm could force the waves as high as a hundred feet or more. He had to act now. He turned sharply.

"Douglas," he called, "here if you will."

The first mate strode to the captain's side.

"Look, mate," he commanded as he pointed to the horizon. "There's a storm brewing. We're in trouble."

Douglas was silent. He also knew the terror of rounding Cape Horn. "I'd say she'll hit in twelve hours. Is everything secure?" checked Palmer.

"I never seen a ship so well gripped, captain. The men have worked well."

"There's more to be done - and that right quickly. First, get two men to cover all glass with boarding. Make sure it's well nailed home. Second, I want lifelines and netting around the rigging and above the gunwales. Third, shorten the watches until she blows. Last, get them to strip her down to the main tops'l and the fores'l. Start immediately. There could be ice on the yards already."

"'Aye, aye, sir."

Douglas left. Matthew Palmer headed for the deckhouse where he instructed Archie to be prepared to put out the stove and lamps in a few hours time. He then went to see the passengers in the poop's stateroom. He told them to remain below decks until further notice. Meanwhile, Jim Douglas led the men in the rigging of the lifelines and netting leaving John Samson and Sandy to board up the windows. These done, they went to furling the highest sails.

As the watches changed, it came on to blow worse and worse. Hail beat furiously upon the ship and stung the faces and hands of the crewmen. The mainsail clapped rapidly as it struggled to be free. The captain ordered it to be stowed next. The men were soon lying over the main yardarm that was encased in thin ice. The skipper knew how hard and dangerous the job would be so he sent the men additional, pliable lengths of rope and told them to tie themselves firmly to the jackstay before grappling with the freezing canvas. The gaskets and ropes at the foot and leach of the sail were as stiff as metal piping and made the work harder. The sailors pounded the sail. Sluggishly, hand over fist, the canvas was pulled up. They had almost dragged it upon the yard when a tremendous gust of wind tore it from them.

Momentarily, the men were caught off balance. The foot rope swayed murderously. A foot slipped. A man screamed. The seamen steadied upon the yard. They turned their heads to see who had gone, knowing that such a fall would be fatal. A remarkable sight met their eyes. There, on the weather-side of the yard, Jed Cole was swinging like a pendulum. Each time he passed below the yard, he grabbed, in vain, at the foot rope above his head. The captain's safety rope held secure. Helping hands soon hoisted him back up onto the yard.

"Thanks," he greeted. "Now I know what monkeys feel like."

"Just as well the skipper gave you a tail then," smiled a colleague. The incident was quickly forgotten as the men again wrestled with the mainsail.

After some time they held it hard upon the yard by leaning over it. The gaskets were flailed, passed around it and, with difficulty, knotted. The frozen seamen unhitched themselves and carefully descended. The third officer checked the knots.

Palmer ordered them to the deckhouse to thaw out. He called out Sandy's watch. They had similar problems when stowing the foresail. However, by one watch on, and one watch off, the Falcon was bared to fore and main topsails. These steadied the ship and prevented excessive rolling.

Suddenly, a squall blasted the fore-topsail from its bolt ropes. The gale was rapidly becoming a hurricane. Both watches were ordered out to stow the frenzied canvas. As the main deck was now continually flooded, several seamen led the required braces to the poop deck. Two men attended the helm. Palmer needed more men. However, he decided against releasing the mutineers. Sandy added to his problems. The mountainous seas and the roar of the wind terrified the boy. The cold pierced him to the marrow. Falcon's master spotted his state and ordered him below. The lad obeyed.

One lamp shone below. Its dull light picked out the rolling shadows of the passengers whose voices pretended nonchalance, but their faces showed fear. Sandy settled himself at a table in a dark corner.

"Lord," he prayed "I'm scared. I've never been as scared before. Even more scared than when Tom Parker pulled out that dead rattler and hung it about my neck. Lord, I haven't asked much of you before 'cause I always had the doctor. But now I've no one but you to turn to. I guess you've got the power to save us 'cause you saved them fishermen in the boat that time. Aye, the winds and the waves obey you, Lord. Could you have a word with them now?"

Sandy paused. The ship continued to rise and dive, the hail hammered the deck overhead, and the wind bellowed threateningly.

"I know that we've got to die sometime, Lord," he continued. "Like Archie said, it's 'cause of sin. I've sinned bad, Lord. I've done loads of wrong things. Some of them, I couldn't help doing. They just happened. Still I guess I deserve what's coming to me..."

The door of the companionway flew open. Archie turned inside and closed it. He then clambered down shaking his hands at his sides.

"Captain sent me to see if all be well. Any problems?"

Nobody replied. Archie recognised the signs of fear. "Don't ye worry," he reassured, "We've a fine ship, and the best captain as ever sailed the oceans."

Sandy caught his eye. The sail-maker winked as he approached the lad. "Art thou scared, lad?" he whispered as he sat down.

"Scared stiff," admitted Sandy.

"What frightens thou most? The sea? The wind? Drowning?"

"All of them, I suppose. But most of all, I'm scared of what might follow."

"What's that, lad?"

'The doctor often told us of judgement. God's judgement."

"He's right. There is a judgement. Good Book says so." Archie ferreted around under his oilskins. He brought out his Bible and thumbed through well-worn pages.

"It is appointed unto man once," he read, "to die and after this the judgement." The sail-maker flicked through the pages again. "Thou need not fear the judgement, lad," he comforted. "Listen to this... There is therefore now no condemnation to them which are in Christ Jesus."

"What's condemnation?" asked Sandy, screwing up his face.

"Judgement. Be the same word as judgement. No judgement for those who trust in Jesus."

"You mean that we can escape judgement?"

"Aye, lad. But only if thou'lt stand where the fire's been," warned the shellac.

"I don't understand, Archie."

"Look, lad. There was once a greenhorn who got himself caught in a prairie fire. He spurred his horse in an effort to outrun it, but the horse collapsed. He shot it and ran on. All the time the fire was gainin' on him. It weren't long before he collapsed. He gave himself up as dead. Then, out of nowhere, appeared an Apache Indian. Instead of scalping his enemy, the Indian did a strange thing. He ran to the fire with a handful of prairie grass. He lit this torch and raced back to set fire to the scrub in front of the fallen man. The wind pushed the flames away from them, leavin' a black, scorched area. The native then lifted that cowboy and put him where his own fire had been. When the other inferno reached the burned area, it had nothing to feed on and petered out. Well, that fire be like God's judgement, and it be after all of us. But that punishment once fell on another un - God's own Son, Jesus, when he hung there on Calvary's cross. So, if we trust that He took our judgement there we be safe, or standin' where the fire's been. Dost thou see?"

"You mean that God punished His own Son for the things that I've done bad, instead of punishing me?" suggested Sandy.

"Exactly. Now thou canst believe it and be saved or throw it back into God's teeth and take the consequences."

"I've never heard it like that before, Archie. I reckon I'll take it. Thanks Archie."

The sail-maker beamed as he gripped the boy's shoulder. "If thou'rt really sincere in what thou'st just said then thou'lt live thy life for the one who gave his own for thee. Thou'lt have peace with God, and thou'lt need fear no thing or man again."

The old sea dog picked up his Bible and left. The sounds of the storm seemed less threatening now. Sandy felt as if a great burden had been lifted from his back, but he didn't know whether to laugh or cry. Instead, he went out to face the storm. He reported to the captain, who, noting that the fear had left the boy's face, ordered him to help the helmsman.

"Iceberg off the port bow, sir." reported the second officer shortly afterwards. Palmer peered through the blistering hail. A dark shape loomed up ahead.

"Man the braces!" he cried. "Brace square!"

The men scurried to their posts. "Helm, ease her slowly to starboard. We'll change tack. Be careful. We don't want to end up on our beam ends." The captain ordered a lookout forward as the high wind shook the main topsail whose yard was hauled square. Then, as the ship came about, the canvas blew back into the mast and stalled the ship.

"Brace in to starboard!" rapped another order. "Hard down on the helm!"

The sail filled again with the wind. The Falcon bit into the oncoming waves and headed to the Northwest and away from the iceberg.

For twenty-four hours the storm clawed at the clipper, but she was hardly scratched. Her wily skipper seemed to anticipate and avoid every attack. Everything and every man was held secure. The wind dropped and the waves shrunk. The dark, molten sky was replaced with a steady grey. Matthew Palmer had again taken on and defeated Cape Horn. Ever mindful of his crew, he ordered the cook to prepare piping hot stew for them.

The Captain turned to Sandy who was just about standing. "Scott," he ordered, "go below and get dry clothes on. Then, if you can make it, get to the deckhouse for some grub."

"Aye, sir," came a dazed reply. "Oh. By the way, how did you overcome your fear?" asked the captain as the boy went past.

"I just stood where the fire had been," answered the youth. "Uugh," grunted Palmer, "what fire?"

Chapter 10.
"A good name is rather to be chosen than great riches" Proverbs 22:1.

With Cape Horn behind them the ship's company was in good spirits. They now respected their skipper and had full confidence in their ship.

"Flare, ho!" cried the lookout from the top of the main mast pointing forward. "Two boats ahead – a little t'starboard."

Picking up his telescope, Palmer went forward. He peered into the ocean ahead. Sure enough, there were two boats. They were tied together and, with oars shipped, were drifting on the current. The figures in them were slumped over except for one or two who waved feebly.

"What is it, cap'n?" asked the mate.

Palmer had only once seen boats bound together like this. Those had contained survivors from a wreck. This looked similar. "Looks like survivors in lifeboats," he murmured. "Launch a boat, Jim. We'll get a tow rope out to them and bring 'em aboard."

With that, Palmer went to the helm and changed course slightly. He ordered a capstan to be prepared for towing and for the doctor and carpenter to prepare make-shift bunks in the saloon.

Meanwhile, the first mate selected five of the crew and quickly prepared and lowered a boat. They were soon inside and ready to row. The mate wound out a number of coils of the towing rope that now lay in the boat's stern and threw them up to Sandy. The rope unwound as it flew. The boy caught it, threaded it through the pulley Archie handed him and gave the loose end to the Old Sage who bound it to one of the capstans.

Archie hooked the pulley to the nearest mast.

At the mate's command, the sailors rowed hard and quickly. The towrope snaked out over the small waves behind them. Jim Douglas watched carefully as it unwound. As soon as they were in throwing distance of the leading boat of survivors, Douglas threw them the line. A couple of exhausted men managed to retrieve it and tied it to the top part of the bow stem. The mate threw the rest of the rope into the sea and rowed round to the second boat. He threw a shorter line to its stern commanding the people on board to make it fast. Wearily they did so. The other end was bound to Falcon's boat.

It was not long before the towrope snapped taut. The three boats were pulled along by it, matching the speed of the Falcon. The sailors winding the capstan slowly wound in the rope and boats. Once alongside, the front and rear boats were tied to the Falcon. The middle boat was lifted aboard and the people, craving water, were helped away by the doctor and a few hands. When the leading boat was hoisted aboard, Palmer was handed a logbook by a middle-aged man whose mouth was so dry and swollen he could not speak. The captain of the Falcon took it and nodded his thanks. The front cover told him that the log belonged to a ship called "Mermaid". Opening it, he found that its captain was Ernest Robert Bowles. He closed the book and praised his crew for their quick work. He then told them where to lash the extra boats so they would not distort the trim of the ship or block major routes of access.

Matt Palmer then went to his cabin to examine the log more closely. It soon became apparent that the "Mermaid" had been heading for San Francisco with a cargo of whale oil and a number of passengers. Almost fourteen days previously, she had felt a severe shudder that was attributed to a heavy wave striking the ship. No damage had been apparent and the normal course of pumping the bilges revealed only the usual amount of water. However, that was not the case a day later. The pumping in the morning continually spewed out water. The well of the ship was sounded and four feet of water was found in the hold. All hands were then set to the pumps and a search was made for the leak. It soon became clear that the cutwater and part of the main stem had been ripped away.

By that time the sea was running high and the ship was pitching violently. Frantically, crew attempted to block the leak under the supervision of a couple of officers, but all to no avail. Captain Bowles had then told his crew and passengers to prepare for the worst.

Within twenty-four hours, the four lifeboats had been launched and the Mermaid was left to her doom. The winds and waves battered the lifeboats and two were overturned and lost. Twelve hours passed before the sea calmed. It was only then that the two remaining boats had been brought together again.

During the days that followed, they attempted to make land, but the currents proved to be too strong. The men grew weaker by the hour and exposure to the elements took its toll. For the last few days, they had left themselves to the mercy of the sea. The drinking water had run dry and the eating of food was impossible because of sore mouths, swollen tongues and rasping throats.

"The sea can be a cruel mistress," groaned the captain of the Falcon closing the book. "I'd better see how the survivors are doing." He left his cabin and headed for the saloon where he found a number of survivors already sitting up and talking together. However, most lay asleep on the thin mattresses provided by the doctor. A number of passengers were helping others by feeding them a weak soup specially prepared by the cook.

The doctor approached his captain. "Looks like we caught 'em in time," he said. "Should all be as right as rain in a week or two."

Palmer nodded his head. "Thank the Lord," he said. Then added, "How many are there?"

"Twelve crew and sixteen passengers," replied the doctor.

"Thanks, Ned," said the captain, laying a hand on the shoulder of the healer. "Where's their captain?"

The physician pointed in the direction of the man who had given him the logbook. "Likes to be called Ernie," he said.

Palmer walked over to his bunk and knelt down. "Cap'n Bowles?" he asked. Hoarsely, the sailor acknowledged his name. He then thanked Palmer for saving them.

The Falcon's skipper told him that he had read the log and expressed his deep sorrow. Tears welled up in the eyes of the Mermaid's captain. "Lost thirty passengers," he said. "Thirty – and crew aplenty."

Palmer sucked in his lips and dropped his gaze. He knew the incident would haunt this man day and night for the rest of his life. Every day, he would question his own actions. "What d'you think caused the damage?" asked Palmer.

"Ice!" he exclaimed. "Ice floatin' under the surface."

Palmer agreed. Icebergs like this were the devil's own shadow to see under the water. He told his fellow to rest and went up on deck. There he called for his first mate and told him to find out how many of the surviving crew would like to help sail the Falcon. These would ease the heavy burden inflicted by the absence of the would-be mutineers. He also asked him to make a record of those passengers who wished to go on to San Francisco. Jim Douglas set about the task. Palmer, himself, went to see the cook.

Chapter 11:
"All things work together for good to them that love God" Romans 8: 28.

Captain Palmer noticed the complete change of heart of his crew following the rescue of souls from the Mermaid. They each had a personal pride in their achievement and it showed. As all the survivors of the Mermaid had agreed to stay on board and the Falcon carried sufficient food and water for them, Matt Palmer suggested that they try in earnest for a record run. He explained that it would give purpose to their everyday work. As the complement of the Mermaid also volunteered their help, the men approved with a rousing cheer. The race was on!

The West Wind Drift and the Westerlies pushed the clipper northwards to the Chilean coast. Falcon then spread her wings by setting her studding sails and flew N.E. with the S.E. Trades.

Progress was too good to be true, that is, until a clear, sun-filled day suddenly turned dark. The Falcon had been flying along under a full array of canvas when the wind suddenly rose to gale force. The passengers were ordered below decks to their staterooms. The wind continued to strengthen so swiftly that Palmer ordered the sky and studding sails to be brought in and the fore and mizzen topsails to be reefed down with haste. However, no sooner had crewmen begun to climb the rigging when there was a phenomenal gust of wind. A resounding CRACK ripped through the ship! This was chased by a heavy CRASH! The ship's fore topgallant mast had broken and toppled forwards to catch on the rigging of the jibsails. It had taken a royal and skysail with it. Fortunately, nobody had been injured by falling debris.

Immediately, the captain rasped out new orders. He knew that a falling mast could cause immense damage and even lead to the sinking of the ship. The more experienced of the crew set about untangling ropes and lowering spars, sails and pulleys. The task was made more difficult by the rolling of the ship that sought to tear them from the rigging. Yet, in only the worst of tangles were they allowed to cut away any ropes. It was a slow and painful process. Meanwhile, other sailors took in the unhindered sails. Then, with the ship more stable and most of the wreckage cleared, the sailors focussed their attention on lowering the broken mast itself.

The heavy timber was inched to the deck with the care and precision that would have made any captain proud. Soon as all the parts were laid out on the deck. Matt Palmer scrutinised each piece in turn. He was thankful most of the spars and sails were undamaged and could be used again. The broken mast could not. He ordered the necessary repairs to the mast that would engage both the carpenter and the blacksmith for a good while. Additionally, he instructed his officers to thoroughly examine the mainmast and its rigging for damage, but to increase sail where possible as the wind had since slackened again.

The ship was put to rights within forty-eight hours and the days that followed were trouble-free. It was during these days that the sailors often talked excitedly about the glittering gold of California. Jedidiah Cole was particularly keen to get to the diggings.

"I bin studyin' the development o' the Gold Rush since it began," he related one evening. "It were Monday, January 24th. when gold were accidently found at a sawmill fifty miles north of Sutter's Fort. The boss o' the mill found it. Marshall were his name. Anyway, he rode to the fort and told his partner, Sutter, about the find. Well, they tested the gold that he'd brought and found it to be the real thing. At first they tried to keep the find a secret 'cause they had no legal title to the land it were on. Bigler, one of the hands, got gold fever and was first to let the cat out o' the bag. Others did the same, and on March 15th., 1848, the Californian newspaper reported the find. That started the ball rollin'. San Francisco heard the news and the male population dropped by near a hundred per cent as treasure seekers swept into the hills. Soon the whole country was resounding with the words GOLD! GOLD! Some reported that the ground of California was one vast gold mine where the mineral was picked up in pure lumps. Fathers left wives and children, sailors jumped ship and soldiers deserted to take up a shovel and a tin pan. The fever spread. On the East Coast ships were rapidly built o' green timber in order to take the fortune seekers to San Francisco. Most of

them were lost comin' round the Horn. Others left the ships in the Caribbean and braved malaria by crossin' the Isthmus of Panama.

Many fortunes were made only to be lost in the gambling halls. Prosperous claims were usually jumped. Only a few managed to hang on to their fortunes. Now all but the largest mines have petered out. I'm going there to write a history of the Gold Rush. I need to get there quickly 'cause gold has been discovered in Australia. Most prospectors are clammering to get back east, but there be some heading down under."

Other adventures opened the mouths of seamen as the nights followed days. Sandy was enthralled by the tales, but was overjoyed when the Falcon entered the Golden Gate after only ninety days of sailing.

This was an untouchable achievement and was celebrated accordingly. Even Matthew Palmer had never experienced such a triumphant passage. He expressed this as he wrote his report to the owners.

"San Francisco,

8th June, 1850.
Sirs,
The main details of the passage are as follows:
We left New York on the morning tide of 19th. March. Shortly afterwards we discovered that two of the crew (brothers) had typhoid. One of them lived. The other died on 6th. April and was buried at sea. Prior to that, on 5th April a gang of the crew, led by Ahab Jackson, attempted to take over the ship in order to be rid of the sick men. The mutiny was thwarted. It seems that Jackson is wanted for murder in New York. The mutineers have been handed over to the authorities in San Francisco.
We met with heavy weather around Cape Horn. Nonetheless, we pulled through with minimal damage. It was then that we picked up some survivors of the clipper called "Mermaid". They are now well in body, if not entirely in spirit. The last hop, from the Horn to the Golden Gate, was fast and, except for a broken topgallant mast, uneventful. We completed the voyage in ninety days. A time to be proud of.
Yours,
Matt Palmer (Captain)."

Palmer put down his pen and leaned back into his chair.

"That's one trip that'll never be repeated," he sighed. A timid knock sounded at the door.

"Come in," bawled the captain.

Sheepishly, Sandy stepped inside. "Hello."

"Sandy. Come in," invited Palmer.

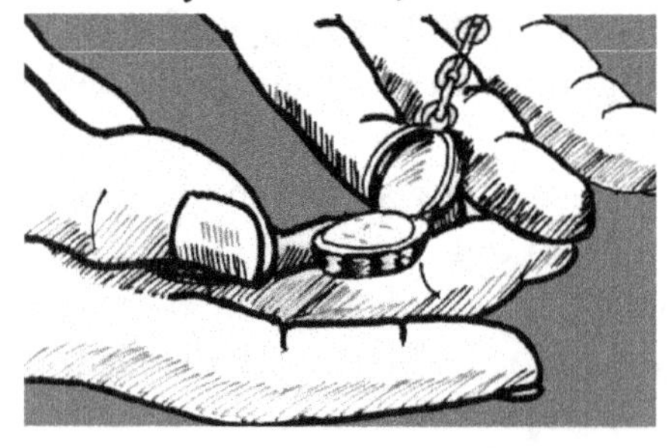

The youth approached his skipper cautiously. "Sorry to trouble you, sir," he blurted out, "but I was wanting t'thank you."

"Sandy, it's been a pleasure to have you aboard, and I hope you'll stick by the sea."

The youth fiddled nervously with something and then thrust his hand towards the captain.

"As a token of my thanks, sir, I'd like you to have this. It ain't much, but it's the most precious thing I've got."

Palmer took the glittering object from the hand of the boy. "Why, thank you, lad. That's very..."

Matthew Palmer paused as he turned the golden locket over in his hands.

54

A puzzled look creased his brow.

"What's wrong, captain?" asked Sandy.

The seaman swiftly stood up. His left hand gripped Sandy's shoulder so hard that the boy winced.

"This locket, lad," he demanded, "where d'you get it?"

Sandy's skin paled. He wondered why this man was so anxious.

"I've always had it," he replied. "The doctor at the orphanage said that it was hanging round my neck when the shepherd found me."

The captain's grip relaxed.

"Sandy, I gave this very locket to my wife for her 25th birthday - see, here's her name engraved - ESTHER."

"Are you sure?" gulped Sandy.

"Positive. My wife and baby son were lost when the Dunstone sank in a storm off Charlestown near fifteen years ago."

"The shepherd found me on a beach north of Charlestown. Does this mean..."

"It means," interrupted the captain as he sat down, "that you MAY be my own son." The captain's eyes glistened as they watered.

"That's incredible!" exclaimed the boy.

"After all these years," mumbled Palmer.

He turned to Sandy, an urgent look upon his face. "I'll have to find out for sure on our return voyage."

"Yes, sir," agreed the teenager with enthusiasm.

"If I may be so bold, sir, you'd make a good father."

Their eyes met as a hammering shook the door. "Enter," called the ship's master.

The mate strode in leaving the door open. "Marshal to see you sir."

"Show him in."

Jim Douglas ushered two men into the cabin. The first was a stocky fellow with a chin blue with bristles. His clothing hung loosely over his tough form, and his tattered hat was pushed back over waves of curling locks. He carried a rifle and wore a badge.

"Aft'noon, Captain Palmer," he greeted touching his hat.

"Marshal Grant," said the captain, "it's good to see you again."

"Likewise." Grant jerked a thumb to his tall, well-dressed, bespectacled companion. "This 'ere's the judge. Judge Bishop."

The captain and judge acknowledged the introduction with a nod. "I just came to tell you that Jackson will probably hang on the evidence of the boy there," continued the marshal. "The torn piece of paper matched the one that

Jackson had. So he must be Crocker's murderer."

"Well, it's good to have that cleared up, Marshal," stated Palmer.

"There's business with the boy, too." Grant's gaze turned towards Sandy.

"Yes, Marshal," said the curious youth.

"Sandy, we telegraphed New York t'see if Jack Crocker had any kinfolk and he ain't. So that leaves us with a problem."

"I don't understand," uttered the boy.

Marshal Grant turned to his fellow. "Judge, you'd best explain it."

The Judge's soft voice was music compared to the marshal's gruffness. "Sandy, the paper stolen from Jack Crocker was the title deed to a gold mine, here, at a place called Crimson Creek. The document declares that the holder of it is the owner of the mine. Ahab Jackson knew that the mine was full of gold and murdered Crocker to get ownership. As Jackson is likely to hang, and the miners tell us Crocker has no heir, we had to decide what to do about the mine. We think that as you had the signed half of the paper, it should go to you."

"You're making me the owner of a gold mine!" spluttered Sandy.

"More than that, boy!" declared the marshal. "The speed the gold's still comin' out of that mine, you'll be a millionaire."

Sandy was stunned.

"Well, what d'you say, Sandy?" asked the captain sadly.

The youth turned to the judge. "Are you absolutely sure that I own this mine?"

"Sure as can be," he stated. "The mine is yours."

"If it's mine, could I give it away?" asked Sandy boldly.

"Give it away!" barked the marshal. "Here now, boy, think what your sayin'. Give it away indeed!"

"Marshal!" rebuked the judge. He then addressed the lad, "Sandy, if you really want to, you may give it away."

"What've you in mind, lad?" enquired Palmer.

"Well, sir," he answered, "I'd like to give it to the orphanage in New York. The one the doctor runs. I owe him so much."

The marshal shifted uncomfortably. He felt ashamed. Meanwhile, Judge Bishop took Sandy's hand and shook it with vigour.

"That's a wonderful gesture, son," he commended. "An investment in lives! We'll make sure that it's done. Come to my office tomorrow morning."

Bishop tapped the daydreaming marshal on the shoulder. "Come on, marshal. Time to go."

They exchanged farewells and the lawmen left. Captain Palmer spoke to Sandy, "You know, Sandy, any man alive would be glad to have you for a son."

"If you'll have me, sir, I'll sail with you."

"I'll have you, boy! And sail we will!"

Matthew Palmer rose from his seat and, putting his arm about the boy's shoulder, headed for the main deck.

The mate hesitated. He was bewildered. "Hey, Captain," he called, "I thought you were swallowin' the anchor."

"Mind your mouth, Douglas!" roared the skipper.

"I've a record breaking clipper and a new life to lead. God be praised! Swallow the anchor indeed!"

They went on together. The mate shook his head and scurried after them, shouting, "'Ere, skipper. Wait for me!"

The Author.

George Stevens was born in the City of Bath. His education was spent in the same city before spending a year at an art college. 

He then decided to train as a teacher and went on to teach at the primary level for about thirty-two years.

During this time, he produced many plays for a variety of occasions and even wrote some of them himself. He retired from teaching quite recently with the intention taking up writing more seriously.

This book bears a Christian bias and is written for children between the ages of eight and fourteen years.

The characters in the book are purely fictional. However, some of the events that occur in the story were common to clipper ships of that period. After writing this book, the author discovered that there had been an actual clipper called "Falcon". It was a fully rigged wooden clipper ship built in 1859 by Robert Steele & Co., Greenock. The use of the ship's name in this story is purely coincidental.

Extra!

The author has produced another book that is based on his own life as a boy, but with one vital difference – a red rubber ball. The "power" of this ball turns the ordinary life of George into one of suspense and adventure. It is called "The Adventures of the Red Rubber Ball" and is aimed at the 6-11 years age range

Hopefully, a further book will soon become available again. It is a play for children of junior age and entitled: "The Pied Piper of Hamelin".